Elisabeth Seale Carnall
24 XII 94
Cambridge
Magdalen Bridge Street;

THE PHILOSOPHERS

THE PHILOSOPHERS

Alex Comfort

Duckworth

First published in 1989 by
Gerald Duckworth & Co. Ltd.
The Old Piano Factory
43 Gloucester Crescent, London NW1

© 1989 by Books and Broadcasts, Inc.

ISBN 0 7156 2511 X

British Library Cataloguing in Publication Data

Comfort, Alex, *1920–*
The philosophers.
I. Title
823′.914 [J]

ISBN 0-7156-2511-X

Photoset in North Wales by
Derek Doyle & Associates, Mold, Clwyd
Printed and bound in Great Britain by
Billing & Sons Ltd, Worcester

1

Went to visit my father. Not a very happy occasion. They are enormously kind and welcoming as always. They act as if I had just left, or was home from school – interested in what if anything I am doing (a little pressure here: our son ought to be doing something as we understand doing something. I think they still hope I will recover). Philosophy, teaching, writing are not doing something. The disappointment shows. Father is strong, busy, pompous as ever, and happy with it. He is seeing England made over in his own image: Mother is outside all this – I suppose she is used to him. I go to see her, I visit him.

There was the usual gracious living dinner: they live like this, they always have done since my father scored. They don't lay it on for me. So we sit down, the three of us, with Mister Antrobus and the secretary. I think they probably invited Antrobus to show me to him once again. He is the partner, the JP, the other half, the one who agrees with Father and I suspect runs him, who lets him win at golf. It is quite difficult, in Spivsville, to go over the line, but if Father ever does go over it Antrobus will have pushed him. He will be in Marbella while Father faces the music. After I've gone he'll give his impressions.

The secretary is something else. She lives with them, en famille, and goes up to the Tower of Babel every day with Father. She comes back with him in the evenings. I suppose they do some work. Sarah, her name is. Long black hair, trousers – you can see how firm she is and the amount of space between her thighs, one of those women you need not undress to fill in the invisible portions. She is modest, reserved and professionally correct, and unlike Antrobus, old boy, she actually disagrees with Father, but she won't meet my eye for long. Eye-contact only with Father. You don't bring a woman like that into the house to type letters. Mother loves her, and treats her like a daughter, but Mother has survived all these years by blanking things out. I'm sorry for Mother, but there is nothing I could do which she would appreciate. Let them keep their equilibrium: the alternative would be chaos.

They have a Vietnamese couple who manage things, probably pretty glad to have fallen on their feet, though Father and Antrobus discuss them as if they were deaf mutes – we've got too many immigrants, but Antrobus has to admit they're damned useful now English girls would rather be single mothers and live on social security instead of helping out. Besides, though you wouldn't know it, he was a Major in Ngo Din Diem's army – had to run for his life when America pulled out, so Father thought he deserved a break, and they must say the couple have made a great adjustment. They used to be quite important people. They can't ever go back, of course. Antrobus didn't think they would want to: after all, they were sitting pretty. Yes, said Mother, it had turned out very well for everyone. I watched the Vietnamese lady's face as she served the duck, but I couldn't tell if it was sad, or deeply angry, or relieved.

'Still teaching philosophy?' asked Father, over coffee. And Mother echoed him, to Antrobus, 'David's teaching philosophy.'

'Oh,' said Antrobus, 'yes.' He didn't ask if it paid well. Probably imagined the old man was financing me, which he isn't.

'What sort of things?' said Antrobus. 'Can't say I know much about it.' Picture explaining to Antrobus why quantum physics has upset the idealist-realist divide. I played it safe and told him it was the discipline of knowledge.

Took my leave about ten, embraced both of them, shook hands with Antrobus and Sarah – momentary eye-contact this time which said, 'Thank you for staying mum.' The red sports car next to my Volkswagen probably belonged to her.

Woken by screams, shouts, fire bells. Somebody had set fire to the Roys' house. The brigade got there before I could. There was no way I could get in and help, but they had breathing apparatus. One of them brought down a smoking bundle, which had to be Mrs Roy – Ajit worked nights. It was lucky she was unconscious, because none of the three kids got out. Mansur Singh was there in the crowd, turbanned and soldierly as ever, even though they'd got him out of bed, and I left him to face Ajit when he got home – we didn't know precisely where he worked, so we couldn't break the news by phone.

'I will support him,' said Mansur. 'He can come to us. This is the third time.'

'The third time?'

'That they have set fire to the shop. Now they have succeeded. If the woman dies, I will find them personally.'

I knew the ambulance would have gone to St Francis, so I got in the car and followed it, to speak to Doc Wiston. Mrs Roy was beautiful, and quiet, and had very little English, only Bengali, but a very sweet nonflirtatious smile, so that we communicated without talking. In Casualty they were clearing up some gauzy ashes with gold thread in them. I sat down on the bench and was asked if I was a relative. I wasn't, and I knew Dr Wiston would have his hands full. I'd see him when he'd finished whatever he had to do.

It was over an hour before Dr Wiston came out. 'David,' he said, 'You came with the Indian woman?'

'Not with her, after her. How is she?'

'Not good. Thirty per cent burns, lung damage. She's lost all her hair.'

'And three children,' I said. Through the glass door I saw a gurney going to the burns unit. There was a drip set up on a stand. On the pillow was a scabby red ball – Mrs Roy's beautiful head.

'Was that another?' said Wiston.

7

'At the third try.'

'Somebody has to do something,' he said. 'I can't, David, but somebody has to do something. It's a bland, blank wall. My God, if I wasn't a doctor I'd be a vigilante.'

'It's an ethical loss, being a doctor,' I said. 'Like being a physical coward, which I am. Except you make a definite choice. If one of the thugs comes in you treat him too. Don't underrate it – someone has to take that line if we're to stay civilised.'

'Stay what?' said Wiston. He and I had been at Cambridge together. I knew exactly where he was coming from. It had been a choice: one of the two possible choices. The third, going along with things, isn't a choice. I'd taken the other, and philosophers don't have a Hippocratic Oath. They have to work out the rules as they go. I think a lot passed between us that wasn't said.

'I've got to go back,' said Wiston.

'Will she live?'

'Probably – if that's a good thing.' He went back through the glass door.

When I got back, number 16 was still smoking. No sign of Ajit – Mansur's wife had taken him away. There was a fire tender damping down, a police car, and a superintendent and a sergeant surrounded by a crowd, mostly Asians. The super was having a hard time. He was saying, 'Now quiet, please, everyone. We don't know the cause of the fire, and we intend to find out.'

Mansur was keeping his temper, very quiet, very reasonable. 'Inspector,' he said, 'we know the cause of the fire. It is the third time they have done this. We have heard the petrol bomb. We have already made two statements. What has been done by you? We would simply like to know which of us is going to be next. Can you tell us that?'

'The fire investigators will be coming any minute,' said the super. 'If you know anything, we shall want a statement.'

'We know,' said Mansur, 'that this is again a racial attack. We know who did it. We know also the public house where they meet, and so do the police – is that not true?'

'We don't even know the fire was deliberately started,' said the super, wearily, 'so it really isn't helpful to talk about racial attacks.' I don't think he liked Mansur calling him Inspector. No sign of the local man, PC Ogden, who is a pretty good scout and would have at least listened.

'We ask simply,' said Mansur, politely, 'if you are going to deal with these people, or whether we must do it.'

The super looked grave, and the sergeant still graver. 'Please leave this matter to us,' said the super, 'and don't anybody even think of taking the law into their own hands. It will be fully investigated. You have my word.'

'It was fully investigated the last two times,' said Mansur, 'was it not, brothers?' Shouts of support from behind him.

The super got into his car in a hurry, leaving the sergeant to move us all on.

When we had got rid of the policeman, Mansur and I walked off together, away from his house.

'You can't do it now, Mansur, you've fingered yourself,' I said to him. 'That wasn't brilliant.'

'I have to do it,' said Mansur. 'It is for one man. No conspirators – they talk.'

'Quite. It's for one man, but you can't do it. You've got a wife.'

'So had Ajit. Also I am a Sikh. These Bengali people do not defend themselves.'

'I know you're a Sikh,' I said, 'but be a sensible one. Get a Gurkha if you don't trust Bengalis for desperate deeds.'

'Bengali lawyers, yes,' said Mansur, 'but for this thing, no.'

'Moreover, if any Asian does anything, guess who will be sent down,' I said. 'Not the National Front. Be reasonable.'

'So?' said Mansur.

'If it has to be done, I'll do it,' I said.

'Why should you involve yourself?'

'Why should you? Same reasons. I saw Mrs Roy at the hospital. If we hit them, the super will have to do something, and he'll be scouring the patch for Asian assassins. I'm white, and you'll be out of town when it goes down. You're still driving parcel vans? Good. Let me know your schedule. We'll give the Law a week in case they do something.'

'They will do nothing,' said Mansur. 'They know very well, and they will do nothing.'

'Have you talked to Oggie?'

'He can do nothing. PC Ogden said so.'

'In that event,' I said, 'I will. A week gives me time to recce.' I thought, this is how one reaches big decisions – by accident, through seeing Mrs Roy's burned sari, not through Cartesian cogitation. An ethical imperative, something Kant learned before he was five.

I really liked my class. Philosophy and psychology are always targets for seekers and worriers, but with this lot I didn't foresee any problems. There were only ten of them, for a start. After a couple of sessions one could size them up: seven of the ten were routine, and I could pinpoint three, two women and a man. Violet was a refugee from parents, getting a degree so that she could teach, blonde, not exactly pretty, but smart, which is always attractive, and taking nothing for granted, which is more so. Sharkey was being paid for by Plessey: he or they had the sense to see that philosophy, not simply mathematical logic but the real stuff, was relevant to computer science. He was disconcerting to teach because he had two states, on and off. He was off a good deal of the time, not idling or losing the thread but quite simply concentrating on something else, and his on condition was palpable – it happened when something which was said happened to fit into his own line of thought. Cynthia was older, about thirty, and less easy to place. She and Sharkey both had protective masks: one was going to have to point them out sooner or later, without getting involved in any psychotherapy. Sharkey was the easier – his protective clothing was the nerd. I could see why he needed it – it enabled him to get on with things without being interrupted or asked to play football. Cynthia's was different, and I couldn't work out how it fitted in – experienced-seductive, knowing, a little mocking, but highly perceptive. If she wanted to play the worldly-wise horizontalist why come to a philosophy class? To pick up the teacher? She did not try, unless asking good questions was her way of doing it.

I asked them at the first class to tell me why they were

10

taking the course. Violet said, 'It interests me, and as I want to teach I need it.' Sharkey said it was obvious, because physics and computer science were going to make philosophy relevant again, and make sense of giving PhDs to science graduates, or didn't I think so? Cynthia didn't answer the question, but said she was a sex counsellor and lecturer, which wasn't what I'd asked her.

The syllabus said 'historical and comparative'. I asked them where they wanted to start. With the Greeks? The Greeks had posed most of the problems.

'We did the Eleatics last term,' said Cynthia. 'Does it really matter where we start?'

I asked her what she had in mind.

'Well, we could discuss any system: the same things would come up, and you could cross-reference them for us. I think the way to do this is actually to do it – to tackle the problems ourselves. If you don't mind teaching like that.'

'Any preference for a particular system?'

'Try us with one which isn't Judaeo-Christian,' said Sharkey. 'I'd choose Buddhism. We don't want one which starts with linguistics or ethics.'

I asked him how he defined philosophy. 'Well,' said Sharkey, 'I'm going to treat it as the search for the algorithm which best describes *alles was der Fall ist*.'

'Right. Who's he quoting?'

'Wittgenstein,' said Cynthia. So Buddhism it was.

It was a stunning three months. Cynthia had been absolutely right – we could have started anywhere, and the three musketeers dragged the rest of the squad along with them. We didn't perceive reality, only phenomena: there were two types of religion, those which didn't comment on the nature of the real, and those which made investigable statements about it, like Buddhism, or science, because that was anthropologically a religion too. When we discussed māya, and explained that the word was cognate with metric and measurement, Sharkey took light and gave the class a concise lecture on quantum mechanics. Then there was Time, part of space-time, and elapsing time, one of Kant's a prioris, located in the brain: Mind, epiphenomenal or primary,

11

Helmholzian or transcendent – in other words, the lot. There were seven people in the class who could write essays showing passable knowledge, and three who were personally engaged in a quest for the Grail. What more could a teacher ask?

After Sharkey had given his own seminars, which included bringing a PC into class and showing how a line automaton could generate a universe, he became dormant again, and I took the chance to introduce historical consequences – how, for example, the same philosophical climate had generated both bodhisattvas and samurai – the ethical and existential consequences of what one conceives reality to be. What, for example, had been the consequences of nineteenth-century positivism?

'It's made us hard,' said Cynthia. 'No teddy bears.'

'In what way hard?'

'It's made us temporary and insignificant. It's made us honest about truth, but it's cut us off from half of human experience.'

'What sort of experience?'

'Experience everyone used to have. Magic, for example.'

'Magic is part of human experience?'

'Of course it is.'

'What exactly do you mean by magic?'

'The sort of – well, mind interactions, which the positivist dogma rules out.'

'Some people would say it also ruled out the idea of living sub specie aeternitatis which preceded positivism. Or rather, it substituted a different species of eternity, right?'

Sharkey suddenly turned on to say that if flowing time was illusory we'd got eternity already, as a fact of experience.

'I take all those points,' I said, 'but I was actually after the kind of effects which going philosophies have on day-to-day living. If you think you'll go to Hell for murdering without subsequent confession, that tends to one sort of behaviour. If you don't, either you find a social rationalisation for not committing murder, or you tend to a different pattern of behaviour.'

'Not being found out,' said Sharkey.

Violet's turn. 'I think there are only two kinds of philosophy,' she said, 'those that give you a second chance and those that don't.'

'Would you like to explain?'

'If you live once, death matters terribly. Whether you think you go to Judgment, or simply that the plug is pulled.'

'Go on.'

'If there's going to be a replay, both for you and for the others ...'

'You mean that belief in serial lives is critical – Buddhism and Hinduism have it, Christianity and positivism don't have it, Judaeism is doubtful, Islam only has it in its Druze version, and that makes a difference.'

'Yes. Well, Hindus realise it – it says so in the Gita.'

Full marks to Cynthia.

'When the killer thinks he kills, and the victim thinks he is slain, both are mistaken.'

'Right.'

'There was no time when I was not, or you, or these princes of men – so Arjuna need not take the battle too seriously? The same could be said for some Christians, you know.'

'But it isn't the same. Heaven and Hell are – well – scary, aren't they?' said Violet. 'Living again would have more impact – it would for me.'

Sharkey, waking up, 'They don't have to be *serial* lives. In fact they can't be. They have to be a coherent superposition.'

Violet, 'It made those military Japanese philosophers pretty bloodthirsty, though. But the Inquisition killed people to save their souls, I suppose.'

Three people talking, seven writing it down. I said, 'Let's hear from someone else. You three do all the talking. Mark, any observations?'

You probably find this tough – I found it exciting. I was doing what Father thought was a non-job. Try getting old boy Antrobus into the discussion. No bottom line.

'I don't have any difficulty with serial lives,' said Cynthia. 'I can remember some of mine. Flashes, of course, not the whole story.'

13

The first reconnaissance was extremely satisfactory. They didn't meet in the pub, but in a sort of annexe next to it, on a corner, facing a blank wall at the side – which was all to the good, because it was going to be possible to take it out without any collateral casualties unless someone happened to be passing down the alleyway. The pub bar would have closed: I checked that the National Front stayed around after drinking hours. The annexe had its own entrance. I thought about wedging the doors shut, but they would almost certainly come out with the blast. Yes, I had a plan of campaign, but it depended on one thing. No, I don't carry contingency planning for this kind of operation in my head. It came together like any other operational theory as I walked past the place. The annexe entrance was up steps – so there had to be a basement. The basement probably had a window – probably barred, so there might be problems there. The window had to be on the alleyway side, if there was a window. One thing yet was needful, or back to the drawing board.

I turned down the alleyway, which was actually a narrow street with pavements. The railings which used to be there were cut down to stumps, probably when they collected railings in World War Two. There was a kind of shallow area, running along the annexe wall, and a big fat cherry laurel, nicely placed. There was a window, very dirty but not barred. There were no lights in the annexe, and the street lamp was on the corner. No problem in nipping behind the laurel, into the area, and shining a pen torch into the cleanest pane. It turned now on one thing. I saw broken chairs, two crates, and some Christmas decorations, and on the opposite wall there was a fattish pipe. I followed it up. There was a meter – QED. I would look a fool if it had turned out to be water, but it wasn't. I had all I needed.

I could see hinges on the window. It opened out, but it was going to be a problem, as I didn't imagine it had been opened in years, and I didn't want too copious an air supply. Nobody saw me resume my walk down the alley, into the next street, and back home. There was a second pub on the way, with a carpark yard in front, where I could leave the VW.

Back in place I made a list. I was going to need a screw wrench, one and a quarter to two inches so far as I could judge. I had that, and a general tool kit for unforeseen operations. I was going to need gloves, surgical or plastic, and a small crowbar in case the window was obstinate. I was going to need a small pot of treacle and a sheet of Kraft paper for when I knocked out the pane over the latch. Those I could get later. The one other thing I needed was an igniter. One thought of the obvious, based on a watch or a 555 chip, but both those would need batteries, and the remains were likely to survive. I really wanted something which would self-destruct. I thought about paper cones full of sand, on the hourglass principle, but these would need a battery and a hot-wire. A fuse would be simpler, and I could light it from outside. But fuses fizz and smell, and the floor overhead seemed to be made of boards. I'd be dealing with arrogant hooligans, who'd be smoking in any case, but it pays to assume the target is both smart and security-minded. If I had to risk lighting anything, what was wrong with a candle, lowered from outside on a longish wire hook? I'd have to bet on gas being a lot lighter than air, so this would be the risky part, but I settled for a candle and substituted nylon line for the wire. That would melt. And I'd put a card sleeve on the candle so that the wick didn't blow out. In fact I'd make a fat candle with a hemispherical base which would stand upright however it landed, like one of those tumble clowns – easily done over the gas stove with a kitchen ladle (remember to wear gloves when making, as wax takes excellent prints). By Wednesday night I had all the gear except the crowbar, and it went nicely in my briefcase. There was room for the class papers.

A spot of bother with Mister Garner, MA, FSA, the genial jackass who functions as our equivalent of academic Dean. Used to be a rabbit in his previous incarnation, one with a ginger moustache and freckles.

'Class going all right, David?'

'So far as I'm concerned, fine. Some very bright folk. I'm thoroughly enjoying myself,' I said.

'So I hear. Not concentrating too much on the bright

15

minority, I hope? Well, I thought I'd mention it. It's one of the weaknesses we have when we're personally dedicated to our subject.' Grin, rabbit-nose, rabbit-nose.

'Somebody complain?' I asked him.

'No. But the back row sometimes feel a bit left out.'

'You mean the seven supply teachers who take it all down and then rule a line under it?'

'They come to learn, you know,' said Garner.

'Well, they do. They've written some damn good class papers.'

'They'd do better still if you involved them more, and didn't hold Socratic discussions with your three disciples who sit in the front row,' said Garner. 'Don't be a snob about supply teachers, David. We've both been supply teachers too. Everyone doesn't have a first.'

Or an MA, FSA, but I didn't say it. 'I'll certainly try to bring the back row in more,' I said, 'but they don't talk easily, and if I throw it to them they simply get embarrassed and lose the point. Honestly, some of them *prefer* to listen. The disciples do as much teaching as I do – more.'

'Well,' said Garner, 'I have to leave it to you. But it's one of the important skills for us, evoking response.' Grin, rabbit-nose. And he lolloped off to find himself a lettuce in the Common Room.

Actually I knew he was dead right. If they are slow I don't have patience. I should teach in parables, not discuss substantive issues with the brightest students. 'Now there were in that city certain racist bastards who oppressed the Lord's people and slew them secretly by night, but Oggie cared for none of these things. And it came to pass that the word of the Lord came to one David, saying, "Take a flaming torch, and when the sons of Belial are met together, consume them with fire." ' The trouble was that I couldn't really telegraph my punches by taking this example, and I didn't know how the parable would end. But it would give them some existential ethics to chew if they could read my mind, God forbid.

D minus one was the next obligatory visit to Father. Mother was delighted as usual, asked what I was doing but didn't wait for an answer. Father was positively genial: he had something in mind. Something which would really interest me: I was knowledgeable about all this computer stuff, wasn't I? Antrobus beamed, which meant he was in it up to the neck and probably suggested it. Sarah looked demurely at her fork – when she looked at me it was guarded: 'If you've rumbled us, please don't say anything.' It turned out to be another version of the old theme – would I come into the firm? There was an ideal opening, if I really understood computers and wasn't just bluffing. I said I'd think it over, as I always did. Antrobus said, 'Mustn't leave it too long, you know. There's competition for this kind of opportunity.' I told them I had a lecture and had to leave early.

The car was in dock, getting checked for next day. I walked to the station. About six streets from Father there was the shore of an enormous wasteland, still guarded by locked gates, but strewn with bricks, glass, the concrete bases of former machine shops, pools of water, some with square edges, others growing algae in craters where something had been torn out. About nine hundred people used to work here making biscuits. Now, apart from a few unauthorised dumps which were moving in from the edges, nothing, except some patches of willowherb reasserting themselves.

I met a solitary policeman, a younger version of Oggie, moving with deliberate speed, and looking, I thought, as if the scenery was getting him down. He met my eye, sussing me out occupationally. I could see him deciding I was boss-class and legitimate.

'What a bloody awful mess,' I said.

'Isn't it?' said the policeman. 'Pretty depressing now, but they're going to redevelop it.'

'Really? What as?'

'That's going to be the biggest shopping centre in the Midlands. Should be really something.'

'Shopping centre?'

'Yes, sir. They're building a sports centre and three

hypermarkets, with parking. I hope they get on with it. I'm tired of walking past that mess.'

'Not making anything, then?'

'Well, probably money.'

'And the stuff in the hypermarkets will be made in Taiwan, or somewhere?'

'You're probably right, Sir. Still, there should be a few jobs going. We need a few jobs up here, you know.'

I knew. I also knew I'd asked a silly question – in Spivsville you don't actually make things, only money, which, as Father and Antrobus never ceased to suggest, was real work.

After the class, Violet asked me if we could have dinner together next day – if it wasn't unethical.

Surprise, surprise. 'Why unethical?' I said. 'I never heard of any rule that instructors couldn't eat with students.' Clumsy way to put it, I realised, but she showed no sign of embarrassment. 'Actually,' I said, 'tomorrow's about the one day I can't manage. What about next week?'

'You don't *have* to accept,' said Violet.

'No, I'd love to. But tomorrow I've got something on, unfortunately.'

'All right, if I can try again.' Exit Violet. Sharkey putting things in his case and grinning like the full moon of May – I glared back. Cynthia had gathered her things and gone, the spear carriers were stumping out studywards. Violet probably hadn't an unworthy thought. I hoped I hadn't upset her, though I couldn't see why I should have done – unless she thought a social invitation had been misunderstood.

2

D-day, double check. Mansur was in Nottingham. I put the briefcase in the front boot of the VW. On the way to the evening class I stopped at a car accessories shop and bought a nice little crowbar, more of a jemmy, ideal for helping accident victims until the Fire Brigade could arrive. We pursued the discussion on Japanese interpretations of Buddhism and read out the essays on the philosophy of the warrior – Cynthia and Vi both very perceptive, Sharkey obviously turned off and thinking about his private world. Vi seemed to have accepted that my refusal wasn't a putdown. I thought she would renew it later.

Went home and ate, checking that the lights in the annexe were on and the pub fully occupied on the way. At about closing time I realised that using the pub carpark wouldn't work after hours – Oggie would check the solitary car. Luckily there was one empty parking space, in the middle of a row of cars which had obviously settled in for the night, so the Force was with me. I took out the briefcase and sauntered off.

I actually met the Force – Oggie on his beat. I waved and he saluted. The target was several streets away and I was a familiar object, case and all. When I sighted it the pub lights were already out and the annexe windows still lighted. Time for a mental check. As I made it, I saw something else beside electric light behind the annexe curtains, an orange flash, followed by a glare, and the windows came out in a fireball. The street was quite quiet, quite empty. Someone had beaten me to it.

But what does one do when a house blows up in a fireball? One goes on automatic. I did – I ran as fast as I could for the annexe door.

Some of the bastards had survived – I could hear clawings and coughings inside the door. Obviously, being who they were, they'd locked it on the inside. Obviously they didn't have the key. But I had the crowbar. I put the briefcase down by the kerb, got it out, and started on the door. It was a really good crowbar. I jumped clear in case the fire billowed out, and three objects fell out on the steps, black, mouthing and barbecued. The fire had very appropriately made them up as blackfaced minstrels – white eyes, fuzzy wigs – and their clothes were smoking. Then the Wild Hunt arrived – fire engine, police car, followed by an ambulance – never saw them so quick off the mark. There was also an instant crowd. The Brigade went in, the libitinarii carted off the three black-faced minstrels, and I stood there like a fool holding my crowbar. There was PC Ogden.

'What happened?'

'Search me.' I hoped he wouldn't. 'I was walking past when the whole place blew up. Luckily I happened to have this – I bought it this morning. Don't usually carry one.'

'Christ,' said Oggie, 'It was bloody lucky you did. Those three wouldn't have stood a chance. Look out!' There was another minor blast inside and two firemen came out like rabbits, shouting through their masks about getting back and petrol bombs in there. The loudspeaker on the police car came on with a crackle and bellowed, 'Everybody back there!' like the voice of God. Oggie pushed me away from the steps, saying he'd need a statement later, the Brigade went in with foam, a blazing petrol can flew out of the upper floor like a firework. I tried to find my briefcase. Somebody in the crowd, however, had pinched it. I was left holding the crowbar.

Cynthia would probably have said that sorcery works, and Ajit, Mansur and I had done it by willpower. I was pretty sure it was cause and effect. The NF had been filling petrol bombs, like the one they used on Ajit's shop, and smoking. Serve them sodding well right, but I had no hand in it – in fact, while on

20

automatic, I'd saved three of the swine, at least temporarily. I hoped they'd need white sticks or wheelchairs. But I was dead sure Mansur would never believe me.

Dr Wiston was the only person I told. In fact, I told him the whole thing, including the way my automatic pilot took over. He understood that bit. He told me it was built in – intention doesn't override sociality, which is as well. They could murder Ajit's kids and maim his wife – I'd quite reasonably decided to barbecue them. 'The difference is that you went on what you call automatic and forced the door, whereas they'd probably have bolted. That's roughly the definition of a sociopath, David. He doesn't go on automatic.'

'You reckon they're sociopaths?'

'The three you let out were unemployed punks, probably looking for peer-group status. But there's a dead greasebag in the mortuary who used to be a prosperous solicitor. He's in all likelihood the sociopath behind the whole business, or he was until he showed them how to make petrol bombs with a cigarette stuck in his mouth. You came out of this with clean hands and a very desirable result, but no thanks to anything but luck.'

'I meant to blow the whole perishing lot of them to Hell and back,' I said, 'and I'd have done it.'

'Well, they spared you the odium and did it themselves,' said Dr Wiston. And he went back to the Sordidness of Cures.

I wished, I wished I could have put it to the class. It was the perfect example of the Twin Interpretations, ahimsa and justice, Joe Wiston and yours truly, the bodhisattva and the ninja, but all I could do was to discuss the dichotomy with more than ordinary feeling. I hadn't done anything, but I would have hated to involve my friends.

Real embarrassment next day. When I came in sight of my digs I saw a slight skidderation outside and adopted a defensive posture, but there was a turban poking out of the hedge, so that was all right. It was only Mansur. I would tell him exactly what happened, and he'd probably say it was divine judgment. When I got to the gate there was a reception committee of three – Mansur with one hand behind him, a

21

second Sikh I didn't know, and little Dr Rajkumar and the herbalist who treated all the Asian wives. Before I could say, 'Hello, Mansur,' he whipped out a garland and hung it round my neck, and all three gave me namasti. Dr Rajkumar had tears running down his face.

'We have one true brother here,' said Mansur. 'None of us in the Asian community will ever forget.'

'Hold it, Mansur,' I said, in a stage whisper, 'I didn't do it. The sods blew themselves up making petrol bombs.'

Mansur gave me a penetrating look. He said, 'Of course. Our lips are sealed, all of us, children too. You, David, should have been a Sikh.'

'Perhaps,' said the other Sikh, 'he has been. It was jolly well done, Mr David.' And they left. No use shouting 'Stop!' and attracting attention. They'd placed the whole little ceremony neatly out of sight of the road. Worse still, every Asian I passed in the road bowed, gave me namasti, or his particular salute. So everybody knew.

Violet's dinner engagement began with the rather difficult problem of transferring it from her premises, where she intended to cook, to mine. On the morning of the appointed day Mansur waylaid me.

'My wife and I would be deeply honoured if you would eat with us in our house.'

'I'd be delighted.' Good opportunity to convince him that I wasn't the local equaliser. 'When?'

'Tonight?'

'I can't tonight, Mansur. I've promised to dine with one of my students.'

'That will be a lady student?'

'As a matter of fact, yes, but …'

'If it was a man student we would be honoured to entertain you both. If it is a lady, you will appreciate privacy.'

'It's not like that, Mansur old scout – I'm not looking over an intended bride.'

'It would be time,' said Mansur, 'in any case, we can still offer some hospitality. You will let my wife prepare the meal.'

22

'I don't think we shall be coming back here. And I couldn't possibly let you put yourselves to such trouble.'

'No trouble, no problem, no refusal. I have your key provided for emergency. We will be invisible. A very fine dinner will be in your refrigerator, only to be heated, not too spicy, and the lady will greatly enjoy.'

'It's uncommonly generous of you, but …'

'I find Panjabi food tastes often better if you give time in refrigerator for the flavours to come out. Only nan will be lacking because that must be fresh, so you will have to take chapatis. We will be happy, the lady visitor will be happy.' I had an awkward feeling that Mansur, who was to my knowledge highly critical of English morals, was putting me on. But there was no stopping him.

'Shall we go?' said Violet, picking up her books.

'Yes, ready. I say, this sounds awful, but would you mind terribly if we eat at my place?'

'No. I was only going to do pasta,' said Violet.

'You see, the thing is, my Indian neighbours heard I was going to have dinner with someone, and they absolutely insisted on preparing an Indian meal as a gift.'

'Nice,' said Violet, 'it goes with the philosophy.'

'I couldn't explain to Mansur Singh,' I began.

'That I'd think curry was an updated version of etchings? Look, David, you don't have designs on me, or I haven't noticed any. I had designs on you, which is why I wanted to meet you socially.'

'Turn right here,' I said. 'What sort of designs?'

'I've had a marvellous time with the group, they've been the liveliest classes I ever attended, and you've done a wonderful job, and I just wanted to have a chance to talk to you without the student-teacher relationship.'

'What I'm like as a person, when I'm not up on the stump?'

'Precisely. I think it's relevant to the ideas. For Christ's sake stop treating me as a dangerous sex object. I'm just interested – it must be tough not letting all those ideas become a handicap.'

'It is,' I said. 'You see how bloody gauche it makes me. You

23

think I'm an idiot off duty and you're probably right. I'm absolutely terrible with people.'

'Not in class you aren't.'

'Not in class because I'm giving out. It's got nothing to do with philosophy, only with being an only child with impossible parents.'

'That makes two of us. I rather hoped philosophy could give me some tips,' said Violet. 'Mine want me to take valium, marry, and replenish the earth, so I left, with the object of being a person. Does that make sense?'

'Very good sense. Mine want me to bow down to the graven image which Nebuchadnezzar the king has set up and replenish my bank account like a good Tory spiv,' I said, 'or rather my father does.'

'That makes it plain sailing,' said Violet. 'Now I suggest we behave like two interesting people and talk normally. Don't you *have* any friends?'

We got to the corner, where Ajit's house used to be. I told Vi that this had been one friend, until his wife was maimed and his kids killed. I hadn't seen him again. The local authority ruled that they didn't have to rehouse him because he had a home – in Calcutta – and was therefore voluntarily homeless.

'Good God,' said Violet, 'did they do anything about the arson attacks?'

'They didn't, but the people who did it blew themselves up with their own petrol bombs a week later.'

What happened to the Roys hit her like a blow. Then she said, 'You're something of a hero to the Asians here, aren't you?'

'Am I? I suppose it's because I get on with them,' I said.

'And they garland you and press dishes on you.'

How did she know about the garlanding business?

'This stinking society,' said Vi, 'does it need bodhisattvas or ninja?'

'Probably both,' I said.

'Which ought we to be?'

'I'm trying to figure that out. Here we are. Let's see what Mrs Mansur has put in the refrigerator.'

'I'm serious. In the class, it sounds as if we ought to be civilised bodhisattvas. People don't burn my neighbours alive, David. These folks need a few ninja – to even things up: it may not sound good in a philosophy paper, and being benignly non-violent's a great let-out for middle-class white talkers, isn't it?'

I told her it was a problem I'd been personally trying to address.

'If you decided to be a ninja I think I'd respect that,' said Vi. 'Were there ninja women?'

I told her I didn't know. There had been Hindu women warriors, mostly Rajputs like the Rani of Jhansi, but Buddhist women were expected to be nuns if anything – I didn't see lady ninja going down well in Japan, but the reasons were cultural not philosophical.

'As they are here,' said Vi.

Later on that evening, after Mrs Mansur Singh's dinner, I told her the whole business. To my relief she didn't find it comic – the tale of the Ineffective Vigilante. Instead she said I had been dead right – both in what I'd intended to do, and in what actually happened. There was some prick of a Cabinet Minister on the box.

'It's not just Asians who need some compassionate ninja,' said Violet.

3

Father had a certain approach, a certain gambit, which always put me on my guard. It was the man-to-man, understanding gambit – well, son David, we've had our differences, but obviously you have to make your own choices even if I don't comprehend them, if you rather leave me labouring along behind you: not that he ever said any of this – the gambit involved implying it, taking it as said. It was invariably the prelude to another bid to see that I didn't make my own choices: it signalled a job, a business opportunity, a niche overseas, or something else which would get me back on the right side of humanity, among the serious makers of an honest fortune. He never gave up on the gambit, no matter how often he saw it countered.

When he moved the first piece on my next visit I thought, 'Not again.' I expected the Antrobus plan to be revived – you've got modern skills which we lack, and we need you to keep the family ship afloat. But a few moves later I spotted a variation. Antrobus still lived, but there was a second project this time.

'Can't be very comfortable, looking after yourself in lodgings,' said Father. Quite unusually he'd got me on his own – no Antrobus, no mother, no Sarah.

'It isn't the Burlington, but I don't like the Burlington,' I said.

'Must be a bit lonely. But I expect you have girl-friends.' The sexual revolution and all that, the lifestyle of dirty nails and many mistresses.

27

'As a matter of fact I've got extremely nice neighbours. They insisted on cooking me a marvellous dinner last night when one of the class came round.'

'You don't have any *problem* with women, do you, David?'

'You mean, do I get my girl students into trouble?' I said. 'No, I don't.'

'I meant,' said Father, 'if you did have any sort of problem with women, David, don't think I would hold it against you.'

'If you mean, am I homosexual,' I said.

'They call it gay nowadays,' said Father.

'I know. And I'm not. All right?'

'Well,' said Father, 'don't mind my question. But I know you, David. After all, your mother and I ...'

'Raised me from the cradle.'

'Quite. And you aren't exctly a self-immolating character. You must need a woman – I did at your age. Why the deuce haven't you found a girl and got married? Too busy screwing around?'

I asked him what sort of life he imagined I led. 'What this boils down to, Father, is that you'd feel less uneasy if I got married. People who screw around, as you elegantly put it, don't necessarily stop when they get married. Now do they?'

'I'm sorry, David,' said Father, 'I put it badly. But you surely have to get married one day. Most normal people do.'

'I agree. No offence – you don't know how I live,' I said, 'any more than you know what I really do for a living.'

'I know what you do, but I can't for the life of me understand why it gives you any satisfaction. Still, that's water under the bridge. You don't understand why I enjoy what I do,' said Father, 'but you can probably understand that I'd like you to have children. It's one way a chap can stay alive, being a grandfather. Or are you too bloody clever to see that?'

'No, I see it,' I said. 'I didn't know you felt like that.' Probably planning a family trust fund.

'Well, I do. I've said my piece. Think about it when you aren't too busy solving the world's problems.'

'You want me to get married?'

'I'd like it. So would your mother.'

'You don't by any chance,' I said, 'have someone in mind? Some poor girl who is longing to get hitched to an uncommercial fellow with no morals?'

'Don't rub it in, David. Even if I deserve it,' said Father. 'But there are plenty of nice women around who have minds which could keep up with yours. Too many of them dashing about kissing frogs who don't turn into princes. But you've got to be rather less boorish with them. When attractive girls look at you, you just glare at them, or go mum, or give a lecture, which is worse. Are you shy under it? I was at your age, damned shy. Hardly dared to tackle your mother.'

'Well, you did tackle her,' I said.

'Eventually. Could have done it sooner.'

'As a matter of interest, Father, when did you observe my unwelcoming behaviour with attractive women?'

'Well, I've seen the way you glare at Sarah Maitland. She's a nice, intelligent, independent, good-looking woman who could probably handle you. You might even enjoy it.'

'Are you suggesting,' I said, 'that I might marry Sarah Maitland?' The enormity of the project which Father had in mind was slowly soaking in.

'Of course not. But you could do a damn sight worse,' he said.

The worst part of this was that Father had thought it up himself, without benefit of Antrobus – a double play: I take Sarah off his hands before some sort of contretemps occurs, and she plaits me back into the Firm. I didn't think even Father had a triple play in mind – that Sarah would still be around when required.

'Well,' I said, 'it's not a bad idea. But from what you said about my lack of come-hither I don't expect she likes me.'

'I don't know,' said Father, 'she's remarkably civil to you – she is to everyone. She may be a bit scared of you of you. But if you were more civil to her I suppose you might find out.'

I hope I dissembled what I was thinking. The really frightening thing was that at dinner Sarah looked at me with something like horror, as if I were Banquo's ghost – the old man had had the nerve to tell her what he was planning. As I passed her, when we got up from table (the ladies in Father's house didn't withdraw, except when Antrobus was there) I saw the back of her ear about a foot away and muttered, 'Don't worry. It's not on.' I got a serious, affectionate look of sheer relief, and Father, who'd been watching me but couldn't hear what I muttered, gave me a beaming smile. Mother too. She didn't know the whole story, but I think Father had suggested me as a nuptial candidate and she was relieved, for quite different reasons.

I hoped Sarah would realise she didn't have to put up with this, because she could blackmail him, and serve him right.

I told Violet about the Sarah conspiracy. I thought she should be exposed to the family background. I don't think it played any part in motivating her to move in: we most certainly liked each other greatly, but even more important she liked the neighbourhood and my friends – the Mansur Singhs, the two Tamil boys, Dr Rajkumar, the West Indian family at the end, next door to what was left of Ajit Roy's shop. There was something here for her. Probably she'd been reared on the outer fringes of Spivsville and found real people refreshing – including Albert and Marie, who'd been in the top floor of No. 24 long before any immigrants arrived. Albert got on famously with them, in spite of calling them 'wogs' to their faces – and minded their children on request, sending them home singing music-hall songs which baffled their parents. Albert had been involved in some capacity in the betting industry, until, according to his own admission, the Cypriots had made it rather rougher than he found acceptable ('I don't mind bricks in socks but I draw the line at bits of barbed wire with 'andles at the ends'), boasted of exploits in the Fringe Economy to the West Indian teenagers whom he taught informally to box, fraternised with PC Ogden, who was familiar with his record but regarded him as a burned-out case, and assured his charges that 'all them cops is bent' – Oggie, of course, excepted. Vi's kind of people? No and yes – she seemed as happy with them as with philosophy, helped Marie with knitting patterns, and could be seen walking down the street, past the broken front walls and the railings Mansur had repainted to look smart and compatible with Sikh-Rajput standards, past the terrible hollow tooth of the Roy's burned shop, like an affable panther in a nature reserve. Albert sparring amicably with Winston Brown, who was three feet taller than he was – Mrs Mansur Singh looking out from behind her net curtains – the Vikramaratne children in numerous hordes – all colourful endangered species, and Violet strolling among them as the queen of the forests which surround the walls of Spivsville. She moved in with me, on affectionate and intimate terms, because I came with the forests.

About a month after she did so, there was a tap at my door, rather too diffident for Mansur: probably one of the Vikramaratne children. I was shaving. I heard Vi going to answer it, colloquy in female voices. Then Violet came back.

'David? Your Sarah's here,' she announced.

'Holy cow! What does she want?'

'I wanted to talk to you,' said Sarah – suit, purse, a visiting migrant from quite another part of the forest. 'I just wanted to thank you.' I think it was the longest consecutive speech she had ever made to me.

'What for?' I said.

'For the way you handled that beastly little plot. I thought you'd better know that I quit next day.'

'Very wise of you, you were being exploited.'

'I know it. I'm not stupid – I've known it all along. But that was the last straw.'

'Being dumped and passed on to me? It's all right, Violet here knows – I told her,' I said. 'Father isn't used to being checkmated. It'll do him good.'

'I liked your father. I thought he liked me,' said Sarah.

'Well, he probably did,' I said, 'but he likes to dispose of people God-fashion.' Probably it was a father she had been looking for, Freud-style, but mine had been the wrong one to choose. 'Are you going to manage all right?' I asked her.

'I'm not unemployable, thank you, David. I've got a job which is confined to office hours.'

31

'Great!' I said.

'With a competitor of your father's and Mister Antrobus's.'

'Still better. Sarah, why don't you blackmail the old goat?' I asked. She looked at me as if she was thinking, 'Don't you be like that too.'

'Ask if you're ever in a jam,' I said, 'come and talk to Vi, and we'll rally round.'

'I'll remember that,' she said. She headed for the door, and was a bit baffled, I think, when Violet embraced her like a sister.

'You told me,' said Mansur, censoriously, 'she was not an intended bride.'

'She wasn't, then.'

'It will be good for you. It will be rewarding to have sons.'

'I might have daughters.'

'That is so. But with sons you could be a strong family, able to do some important things.'

'We are not about,' I said, 'to raise you an army of Rajput vigilantes. In any case it would take too bloody long, even if we start now, which God forbid.'

'One day,' said Mansur, 'you will please explain your very unusual marriage customs. I heard about them from my parents but I did not believe them until I came here. I shall need to warn my daughters, when I have daughters. Or better still send them home.' Mansur had a way of getting the Rajput last word and taking the mickey with it.

He still didn't believe me about the National Front.

32

4

Exam week – Vi left early for the library. As I prepared to start the car, I heard Oggie's measured tread behind me and accelerating.

'Psst. Philosopher,' said Oggie.

'Yes?'

'Look – pass the word there's a bust going down tonight. At the Caribbean Social Club.'

'I'll talk to Winston,' I said. 'Aren't you off limits?'

'I have to walk this beat. Tell them the brass are on the rampage. They're coming in heavy. I'm scared shitless.' Then, fortissimo, 'Good day, Sir, and thank you.' And he accelerated without breaking step. I turned aside into the video arcade looking for Winston Brown. Decent chap, Oggie, and pardonably worried. It's demoralising to have a target painted on your back.

Having tea when the Goons roared in in their chariots – vans, dogs, bullhorns, the entire circus. Winston Brown had his head banged against a wall, and poor old Rajkumar, who was pottering along without an evil thought, was thrown head first into a van and had his spectacles broken. When one of the Sons of Laura Norder realised he was a brown black, not a black black, he was thrown back out on the pavement.

'You should do them too, man,' said Winston, recounting the events of the day. 'Somebody better do them one day.'

'Not so much of the "too", Winnie. I haven't done anybody,' I said. Vi remarked that it was bloody disgusting.

33

'Sure, and it's routine,' said Winston. 'Did you see Oggie? I thought he was going to be very, very sick. I told him, you like your friends? How come you aren't a racist pig, Oggie?'

'Lay off him, Winnie – he tipped us off,' I said. 'He isn't responsible, so don't give him a hard time.'

'Then they go on the box and Chief Constable assures the great British public that they don't pick on black folks.'

'You got it all wrong, Winston,' I said. 'Want to know the real reason? They breed these Dobermanns specially and train them whom to bite. If they see someone with a black face they mistake him for a coalminer – there's nothing racist about it.'

'That's funny,' said Winston, 'but I'm not laughing. These are no dogs.'

'Well,' I said, 'they're sons of bitches, aren't they?'

'I tell you, Dave,' said Winston, 'somebody's going to have to do them, and I ain't joking when I say it. They'll do just one thing too many – right?'

'Right,' I said, 'I'm afraid. And I don't think it's funny – I'm white, and I don't get stopped and hazed every time I go to the store or walk down this street.'

'What I need now,' said Winston, picking up his guitar, 'is a small smoke.'

'Not in here, Winnie, if you don't mind. Knights errant need clean noses. If Oggie smells weed he gets robotic about it.'

'OK, Dave. I go home quietly soon. I take it there's no objection to music?' He looked round as if taking a vote. Winnie was a pretty good poet – not a Bob Marley, but good enough. Violet stood beside him listening, trying to understand Jamaican, trying to understand, trying to come to terms with Spivsville and wondering what had happened to the England on the school maps. Extension studies in philosophy – the applied Unit: not obligatory for credits.

We gave him a hand-clap, and he grinned wearily. 'My head still hurts' he said. 'Look outside, man. See if the motherfuckers have gone yet.'

All my class, including the Silent Majority, did creditably on parade. Even Mister Garner MA, FSA was mildly congratulatory and invited me to dinner (lettuce?) which I declined. Sharkey invited me to a class party ('you and Violet', grinning from ear to ear) which I accepted, chez Sharkey. But when we arrived, there were exactly two people present – Sharkey, striped pullover and spectacles, and Cynthia in a dramatic, green Batman poncho, sitting backwards astride a chair: cheese, biscuits, celery, and a case of Barbican. Sharkey liked his mind clear.

'Where are the others?' I asked.

'Didn't ask them,' said Sharkey. 'This is a philosophers' party.'

'Isn't that a bit elitist?'

'Who cares? They'd only make crumbs.'

Cynthia said something about a Special Relationship. Sharkey started opening cans.

'A toast,' said Sharkey, 'to the ninja sensei.'

'Sensei maybe, but I disclaim ninja.'

'You could have told us about that caper, David,' said Sharkey. 'It was class material. It exactly illustrated what we'd been talking about.'

'Who told *you*?' I said, 'and what?'

'It wasn't a breach of confidence,' said Violet. 'Cynthia heard from the Asian grapevine that you'd wasted the NF headquarters. I thought I ought to put the record straight – you might have had goon trouble. Hope I did right.'

'It was affectionate,' said Cynthia.

'Incidentally, if you want to extend your operations,' said Sharkey, 'I've hacked the racist bulletin-board. You need an intelligence capability.'

Cynthia said I'd succumbed to inferior Benevolence, and she liked that.

At that point Sharkey suddenly became cloudcapped, and didn't re-emerge until we'd eaten most of the food. Then he drew up a chair, sat down heavily, and said, 'I've been thinking operationally about the implications. Suppose Adolf Hitler had been removed from the scene when he showed his true colours – would he have been replaced by somebody less

35

crazy and therefore more dangerous, or would all those people have survived? I wasn't there, but on the picture as I read it, it would have been not only justifiable but a duty to waste him. Wouldn't have been an easy decision then, however, because we know what he did, and one couldn't have been sure what he was going to do, even though he set it all forth.'

'We could be in about the same place now,' said Cynthia.

'We could. But there isn't an Adolf to remove,' said Sharkey.

'I'm sure you got a great deal from the study of Buddhist philosophy, Shark,' I said, 'but not, I would imagine, a rationalisation of terrorism. Or is your family name Bader-Meinhoff?'

'Terrorism,' said Sharkey, 'is, apart from a very limited application, idiotic. It appeals to idiots anyway. They use pounds of jelly to blow up a pylon, instead of two feet of cortex. They antagonise *les gens bien* by wasting innocent characters, which is what generals normally do – after all, governments are the archetypal terrorists, aren't they? They're operationally silly – they send showers of letter bombs, and the first one unmasks all the others. Daft. There haven't been any *intelligent* terrorists.'

'But when the Shark decides to act, look out Thatcher,' said Violet.

'If I thought violence was appropriate,' said Sharkey, 'I'd at least organise it operationally.'

We were used to Sharkey's seminars – I enjoyed them myself.

'First, there would have to be limited identifiable targets. Second, destroying the targets would have to have a high probability of ending an abuse. Your caper was mostly rough justice, David, and that doesn't interest me. Procedure: I would need a support group. I'd pick it very carefully from long-term intimates with appropriate character and skills – you lot might be a field for selection, but I'd have to be damn sure of not getting a mole, and I'm not dead certain of Cynthia there. She could be MI5.'

'Thanks,' said Cynthia.

'I'd then give them a seminar. Methods: why use an acute

36

form of attack, like bombs and bullets, which are the methods they guard against? Use armaments which won't let them know they've been hit until it's too late –'

'Give them AIDS, sew radioactive buttons on their shirts?' said Violet. 'Charming!'

'Precisely. There are two ethnographic techniques of hunting,' said Sharkey, 'stalking and trapping. In stalking, you go to them. In trapping, they come to you. The second requires patience, but it's more reliable.'

'*How* do you know you wouldn't be getting a mole?' said Cynthia, 'apart from leaving me out? Jesus Christ did.'

'He picked too many disciples. End of seminar,' said Sharkey.

'Is there a grain of serious intention in all this garbage, Shark?' I said, 'or are you putting on my teaching methods?'

'As a matter of fact,' said the Shark, 'I thought you'd never ask. Yes, there is. Your immigrant friends need protecting. What is supposed to protect them? Democratic society. What is "democratic society"? Well, it's now run by people who got a 40% vote. They're dedicated to extremist policies but they aren't Nazis. They're slowly imposing censorship, like the late Adolf. They're busting unions, like the late Adolf. They're racists, but more shamefaced about it than the late Adolf. They're recruiting goon squads, like the late Adolf. It already looks like a duck, quacks like a duck, and swims like a duck. In fact it's probably a duckling which has learned from Adolf's mistakes, as far as pillocks can learn. Somebody has to do them.'

'I've heard that before today,' I said. 'Is the argument that we now blow them away?'

'No, it isn't, David. This is the serious part. Ahimsa or justice, bodhisattvas or ninja – why the hell not both? Wise as serpents and harmless as doves. They're pillocks and we're experts, or some of us are – why should experts be baa lambs? You can't *assassinate* a social system, but you can bugger it up, especially when it runs on a technology the palace eunuchs don't understand and you do. Why do you think I took up computers? And came to the classes?'

'I think I see what you're on about, Shark,' I said. 'It's a heavy idea. It deserves thought.'

'To which end, we need a small association of philosophers,' said Sharkey, 'an Invisible College of Rosicrucians, dedicated to ahimsa and Mental Fight. Read your Blake – I think he's one of the most important British philosophers.'

'Right on!' said Cynthia. 'All across the board.'

'And here was I thinking that non-alcoholic beer was going to your head,' I said. 'You're serious.'

'I'm serious.'

'Are you on? For a talking dry run?'

Violet said, 'It won't help the people where we live.'

'Not immediately,' said the Shark. 'Tactically, David did the right thing, even if it didn't come off. If it had come off he'd probably be in the slammer for life and strategically neutralised. We *all* need protecting. That's what I'm saying.'

I looked at Vi, 'You know,' she said, 'he's talking sense with it.'

'Incidentally,' said Sharkey, 'I've got a job.'

'Never,' said Violet, 'selling snake oil?'

'As a matter of fact, yes. I am engaged as chief computer programmer for a major City institution which wants to be abreast of the Big Bang. They've got a cracking good mainframe, lots of facilities, and they know bugger all about computers. I shall be close to the most vital areas of Spivsville.'

'What firm?' I asked, with a slight sinking feeling.

'Knight Hollis and Antrobus.'

'That outfit,' I said, 'belongs to my Father, and he offered me the job of organising you.'

'Which you refused because you didn't see the possibilities,' said Sharkey. 'Sorry, Dave.'

'Don't be,' I said. 'I shall watch your activities with intense satisfaction. It sounds as if you carry on and we watch, though. No need actually to bring us in.'

'Don't be sure,' said Cynthia. 'I might have some lines of action I could develop. May I do a reconnaissance? Some of my friends know the Abominable Snowmen pretty intimately.'

'And we'll need you, if you don't mind, Dave,' said Sharkey, 'as our sensei – to bounce things off you and chew over the implications.'

'Any orders for me, Shark?' said Violet, 'or do I come with the furniture?'

'Well,' said Sharkey, 'you and Dave are one flesh, I rather gather. But don't be silly, Vi – of course we want you. You're one of the Disciples.'

Well, other people have had disciples they didn't bargain for, who gave them ideas they hadn't themselves explored. Sharkey was a comedian, but far more brilliant than I'd recognised, and the nerd is a great protective mask, like the Dispassionate Academic.

When I let slip 'disciples' in front of Mansur, he looked very dubious.

'You are now in business as a guru? You are launching a religion?'

'No way: it's a joke, Mansur – I teach students. I thought you celebrated gurus.'

'We honour our gurus, but we do not have more of them. The last Guru passed on that office to the Holy Book, and that is that. This was a very wise and far-sighted protection against persons rocking the boat.'

'And professors of philosophy?'

'Take remarkably little interest in us. They find other Indian religions more interesting. We are a brotherhood, not a shop for theories. In our Book Sahib there are prayers, not theories.'

'Theories or not,' I said, 'this philosophy lecturer likes your attitude. It makes you pretty good people.'

'Well,' said Mansur, 'you could convert. Especially since you are at a religious loose end – not a Christian, not a Muslim, not a Hindu – but clearly a devout person.'

'There is an insuperable barrier, Mansur,' I said, 'I could never learn to put on a turban and make it look sharp.'

Mansur said it would only take him a week to teach me, and

Violet would need to convert too – that is if we regularised our position. In fact, they'd perform the ceremony down at the gurdwara. Well, it's an option.

5

Three weeks later Wesley Lamont's mother fell down stairs.
Fell, was pushed, was pushed by a detective inspector, was
picked up and thrown downstairs by a detective inspector,
God alone knew, and Oggie, whom I asked as soon as I heard
about it from Winston, hadn't been there.

Winston was as near pale with fury as he could manage.

'Dave, you got any bottles?' he said, when my head came
round the door.

'What sort of bottles?'

'Any sort, man. Wine, beer, milk.'

'What for, Winnie?'

'Ask yourself. The pigs just killed Mrs Lamont. It is one
thing too many.'

'Hey, Winnie, steady; are you sure?' I yelled after him.

'She dead, I am sure of that.' He was off like a hornet before
I could make any further inquiries.

'What was that?' said Vi.

'Winston. He's rounding up bottles. Says the police killed a
Mrs Lamont.'

'What's he want bottles for?'

'Petrol bombs, I imagine. I'm going to find Oggie and see
what the score is – this was bound to happen eventually.'

'I'll come too.'

'You stay here. If the neighbours come round to find out
what goes down, tell them I'm out on recce. It'll help them if
you hold the fort.'

Oggie was on the corner, with his little radio, looking as sick

41

as an aviary full of parrots.

'You know anything about this?' I asked him.

'Only that the heavy mob raided the Lamonts and it went wrong,' said Oggie. 'We told them to leave it to the local nick. Now look at that!'

There was a steady Afro-Caribbean current, twos and threes, not hurrying but going the same way, keeping on the opposite pavement from Oggie and either not looking at him or giving him dirty looks. A couple of the lads, when they got opposite Oggie, happened to spit – not at him, but in front of him.

'Why?' I said.

'Wesley's a villain. The word was he and some friends of his knocked over a jeweller's in Reading. The Yard want to talk to him. So they asked Crime to turn over his mother's place. We told them, "Leave it to us, we know the family." But the super says, "No, he's armed. We'll handle it." Strict orders to the local nick to stay out unless they request a backup.'

'So?'

'They cocked it up – don't ask me what happened. I wasn't there. Nor was Wesley. The place was clean. That's all I know.'

'Can we cool it, officer?'

'If you can, good luck,' said Oggie. 'If you can't, there's going to be bloody mayhem. I hope our super keeps his head and doesn't call for troops. Can't you talk to some of the community leaders?'

'I could try Billie Gross.'

'You do that,' said Oggie. His little radio crackled and told him to come back in sharpish. The Sergeant had looked out and found a crowd gathering.

I didn't need to find Billie, because three minutes later he went past running.

'Don't hold me, Dave,' he said, 'I gotta get there before this town explodes.'

'Find Winston and cool him,' I shouted.

'Will do – but if the Goons come in we're done for.'

He chased after a trio of black kids, put a hand on a

shoulder, and disappeared round the corner in the general direction of the nick. Billie was arguing, the three kids were gesticulating. Old Mr Solomon came out of his furniture shop, took a long look over his spectacles, gave me a prolonged thumbs down, and began lugging a stout collapsible grille over his shop window. Then he gave me a seal-flipper gesture of despair, locked the front door, and hung a closed notice inside the window. If Solomon thought that way he was probably right.

I was right to leave Vi to hold the fort because the flat was packed – Mansur, Mr and Mrs Vikramaratne, Mansur's brother, Dr Rajkumar, assorted children in the hallway.

I told them I didn't think the trouble, if any, would come down the Asian end – the focus would be the Winslow Estate, which was the Afro base. Rajkumar had been sensible to shut up shop, because, on the corner, he was in the line of fire. Mansur promised to look after him, and the Vikramaratnes.

'In any case,' said Mansur's brother, 'we are sending for reinforcements.'

'What reinforcements?'

'Oh, we are organised. We have thirty young Sikhs on standby for occasions like this.'

'I've got tea,' said Violet. Tea! Up the WVS, I thought.

I told Mansur it wouldn't hurt to have his thirty jawans as local stewards, but to keep them off the street and not march them in like an army.

'Oh, no. They will come singly,' said Gurdev Singh, the brother.

'If they attack the Afros,' said Mansur, 'we should not stand aside. It will be our turn next. Now, positioned as we are, we can take them in the rear.'

'Look, Mansur, the objective at the moment is to cool it, let Billie Gross talk to the police, and stop war breaking out. Your mission is to protect your families if anyone runs amok.'

'It is the police I am talking about,' said Mansur.

'I know, I know. But in a riot things get out of hand. Goondas break windows. Every man's hand is against his neighbour. Didn't you ever see that at home?'

43

'At home when there was trouble we knew who was who,' said Gurdev.

'It's less simple here. Stay indoors and keep a sharp lookout. Fill plenty of buckets in case of fire.'

Gurdev, with an air of great seriousness, went out in the hall and came back with a businesslike sword.

'Put that damn thing away,' I said. 'Get lathis if you need a means of persuasion.'

'He is right,' said Mansur. 'If the police see swords, they will turn on us. They will be very excited and revengeful.'

Violet came alongside. 'What's happening, Dave? Is it just a panic or is the Third World War going to break out?'

'Could go either way,' I said. 'There's a protest outside the nick, and Billie Gross is talking to the super. If he cools it, nothing may happen. If the brass decide to send in storm troopers, they'll get a bloody nose and all hell will break lose. Mansur!'

'Dave?'

'I've got a good view from here. There are two two-metre radios in the drawer there – Vi will show you. You take one and I'll keep the other. We'll put them on the call channel. It's illegal, but the cops won't monitor the ham band. If there is a riot, I suggest your chaps close off the end of the street, in a peaceful sort of way, just to make sure the row doesn't come this way. And make damn sure they don't join in. They're disciplined blokes.'

Vi said, 'Are you the commanding officer, Dave?'

'Not if I can help it. Just being helpful. No officers here, eh, Mansur?'

Mansur gave me the Rajput equivalent of a wink. 'No officers – Sir!' he said. 'Probably the English cannot get out of the habit. Personally I do not mind. Dave is our brother and trustworthy.'

'Thanks, Mansur. Now everyone cool down.'

Mansur and Gurdev were anxious, but a bit high with it. Little Mr Vikramaratne was plumb worried, and didn't have enough English to follow the conversation – what he did understand was enough to scare him stiff. Mrs V was a pair of

44

large eyes inside the pallav of her sari. The kids were fooling about on the stairs. Vi filling Mrs V's teacup.

They drifted off as the lunch hour came round and nothing happened. A march went past the end of the road with posters, led by Billie Gross and escorted by Oggie, and that shouted but was peaceable. I thought we'd probably fended off trouble this time. Even Winston, when he popped his head in, seemed to have cooled off and settled for constitutional methods. Vi went back to reading. We ate a very good tinned pie, and I dozed off. The news reported the unfortunate accident to Mrs Lamont, the police explanation, and the Labour MP about to see the Home Secretary. The police were going to inquire into themselves.

About teatime it was as quiet as the grave – absolutely none of the usual comings and goings, but there was a preternatural number of policemen, in pairs. I spotted Oggie, accompanied by a strange constable, and ran down.

'Officer? Just a word.'

'Yes, Sir?'

'Look, things seem to have been defused a bit.'

Oggie didn't look too happy about it.

'My neighbours were a bit worried. Could you pass the word where it matters that the Sikhs aren't in on this? Some of the lads have come to make sure their families are all right, and keep any bother out of the street.'

'They'd far better leave that to us,' said Oggie.

'Oh, they will. But if the police see them around, they don't want to lean on them. They're solid citizens, I know them.'

'Thank you, Sir,' said Oggie. 'I'll pass that information on.' Then, noting that Constable Number Two had moved on a few steps, he muttered, 'Keep your heads down tonight.'

No need for the warning, because at that moment I could hear the chariots of Pharaoh and the horses thereof going past the end of the street, and got back inside as fast as possible.

'Mansur! Do you copy?'

'I copy, go ahead.'

'Goons coming in. Stand to.'

'We are ready. We will not show ourselves.'

'Roger. Good idea. I'll keep an eye open. Out.'

What happened is history. We couldn't see Winslow, except the tops of the tower blocks. We could hear the noise, of course. About seven, red glare started between us and the towers. By half past we could see spots of light from lighted Molotov fuses wobbling down from the tower windows, and there were fire engines. Then we got a clear view of the storm troopers, helmets, shields, the lot, marching across the end of our road, banging on their shields like a Zulu impi. Vi watched them without a word. She'd run out of comment. About twenty minutes later there was a crescendo, then a huge orange fireball right under the towers, and then pandemonium – the storm troops coming back, dragging their wounded, and a huge, hoarse cheer.

'Mansur?'

'Colonel sahib?'

'Stand by to close off the street.'

A couple of dozen Sikhs piled out of Mansur's and nipped into front gardens. Most of them had bits of one-by-one or pieces of fence rail. They weren't needed, because the police parked a bus across the junction. That blocked my view for the rest of the night, but we got no sleep, and neither did the neighbourhood.

In the morning it was quietly smoking. Billie Gross, covered with ashes and smelling of teargas was banging at the door. He was in a state one can only describe as prostrated fury.

We sat him down and gave him tea.

'Bad?'

'It's like a battlefield. This time, we gave them a bloody good hiding.'

Billie, who spent all his time cooling things, running Community Relations, the Police Liaison Committee, transformed by battle into an avenging angel.

Vi and I got the story out of him later, after Mansur and some of the Sikhs came round and returned my handheld radio. When the outriders of the Wild Hunt arrived at Winslow, the kids met them with rocks. They backed off, and the crowd came out after them, setting fires, looting, and pelting the fire brigade. Then the storm troops arrived. Winston and his committee, which included people from black areas where this had happened before, had things organised. Little by little they drew the goons into Walsham Street, which was under fire from one of the towers – they'd chuck a few petrol bombs and retreat before the police could fire gas at them. Finally the riot squad and some mounted officers were a long way into Walsham Street and well packed in. Winston and some friends, who'd been lying doggo on the roof of the pub, lobbed over their own Molotov bombs – not bottles but ten-gallon carboys. It was a massacre.

I understood Winston. This had been brewing up for weeks. I hadn't been picked up six times, or had my head banged against a wall. At the same time, it was bad medicine. I was sorry for the people at the local nick. There were pushers at the Social Club. There were some villains at Winslow. If they'd been white, Oggie and his lot would have dealt with them secundum artem and nobody would have thrown any bombs. I was even sorry for the goons, in view of their casualties. After all, they'd been getting good overtime beating up strikers at no personal risk. This was the first time anyone had given them a plateful back. It was unnecessary – or was it? Billie Gross was coming down, realising the damage. He set off to see the super and try to save something, a bit ashamed at having gone berserk but walking a lot taller. Mansur and the others were admiring, but had the sense to hope that that was that. Joe Wiston spent the whole day treating teargassed babies and old ladies, concussed journalists and goons with burns. Two Tamils who ran the Post Office and had stuck to their post Rajput style were killed when a petrol bomb set the shop on fire. The worst bit of news came in later. Some boys who didn't know him had done Oggie, and he was in a coma with a fractured skull.

I was divided down the middle. The ninja wanted to organise them and teach Spivsville the lesson of its smelly little life. The bodhisattva recognised that this wasn't the way to do it.

6

A new term, a new lot of students: good, but I missed the Three Musketeers – or rather two of them, because Cynthia took the course again.

I don't think the rioting had anything to do with Vi's decision to move on, except that it completed her education. 'You do understand,' she said. 'I've got work to do. I couldn't have done it without what you've given me, David, in the classes and out of them.' But she didn't want to settle down yet – perhaps later, perhaps with me, perhaps with somebody else. Of course I understood.

No word of Sharkey – he hadn't reconvened the Invisible College. Probably forgotten about it.

'I thought,' said Mansur, 'that there was an understanding between you.' Referring, no doubt, to Violet.

'So did I,' I said.

Mansur shook his head and said these things were much better if arranged properly. I accepted an invitation to the gurdwara and sat on the floor while they sang prayers to a harmonium, and Mansur served his guru the Book by fanning it with a flywhisk and paying it the honour due to a teacher.

I don't know if it had soaked in that I had not been the champion of the community, but Mansur didn't hold it against me, and seemed bent on giving me another chance. This one was a lot less desperate. There was a Mr Ramachandra who was an immigrant himself and owned about eight very overcrowded houses. Unfortunately, being a learning type, he'd learned the lessons of Spivsville if he hadn't already

49

studied them back in Bhopal. So he had already acquired a Mercedes, a house in Hampstead, and some very exploitative attitudes towards his tenants – like bringing an Alsatian round when he collected rent, smashing up the plumbing, putting their stuff in the street and changing the locks, all quite legally and all with complete impunity. Anyhow, Mansur decided he was polluting the environment and asked me what we did with him.

I was personally against bombing his house, setting fire to his dog, which wasn't really blameworthy, knowing no better, or cutting his throat from ear to ear. I thought putting the frighteners on him would be quite sufficient, possibly assisted by trashing his car. Oggie was permanently off the Force, so we couldn't complain to him, or any of the huge force of police who now infested the place in spite of Billie Gross's warnings that they were a provocation to more of the same. When he came out in his nice suit accompanied by the dog and a bodyguard, after telling a young woman she would have to pay him off in kind, we surrounded them, with sinister black plastic bags over our heads. Gurdev sprayed the dog's nose with soda water, the bodyguard ran, and we asked Mr Ramachandra whether he preferred to be doused with petrol and ignited, or to be stripped naked and handcuffed to a lamp post. He chose the second, and spent the early part of the night watching his Mercedes burn out. The police were so busy putting out the car fire that they didn't find him for an hour, and it took them another to raise a bolt-cutter. We sent him back his clothes with a cheap rate air ticket in the pocket, and the place knew him no more. I'd no moral qualms about that.

Visiting Father again: I had to listen to a discourse on immigrants, urban riots and hooliganism – not so much racist as anti-foreign. He would have been as voluble if they'd been Frenchmen, and he would have said the same things. Father has something of Mr Punch about him. Mother listened to the familiar discourse. No mention of Sarah, but quite a bit of tension in the air – I'd let the side down and failed to rally round. Antrobus discoursing on niggers, Father trying to moderate his tone and keep it within the bounds of respectable liberal prejudice. He gave up after Antrobus's third Martini, and simply looked helplessly in my direction while I scowled back.

'That job you wouldn't consider, David,' said Father. 'We've recruited an excellent computer man to put us in the picture. You could have been his immediate superior, you realise?'

'He's good?' I said.

'Excellent, from his references – the very best.'

'He should be,' I said. 'I taught him.'

'Taught him what?' said Antrobus, looking suspicious.

'Philosophy. He was in my class.'

'Oh, that,' said Father. 'Well, we hired him as an expert, not a philosopher, I'm afraid. He's doing extremely well.' I expressed the hope that it would be a fine morning for him. Sharkey was evidently dormant, i.e. not talking at the moment, but I could afford to wait with interest and hear what atrocity he was planning.

The new class was quite different but just as good as the last – better, in fact, because there were no walk-on parts. I had only eight students (Mister Garner came out of his burrow and gibbered a bit over low numbers) but they were quality – four mathematical physicists, a very bright Indian organic chemist called Sarkar, Cynthia as chorus from last session – still a bit of a puzzle, was Cynthia – and two larval priests, Fathers Malachi and Matthew – pink, shiny, but extremely sharp. I reckoned they were officer cadets for the Catholic SAS.

No historical studies this time – the physicists took over and ran with it, so we started on the implications of quantum physics and the observer paradox for Mind – allusions to Nagarjuna, Kant and the Eleatics came up by themselves as we wrestled. In other words, I taught this course the other way around. The two Rev. M's were in there pitching before you could say Papal Infallibility, and they played with a hard ball – no Thomism, in fact it was Fr Malachi who said that in view of what we were saying about causality as against

51

correlation, First Causes were old hat at the original Thomist level. Cynthia was quite unusually quiet, taking very little part in the writing-up of algebras on the blackboards. She seemed to be eyeing the two pink celibates as if they were scampi – deciding which one to eat first. But her behaviour was wholly correct. She didn't emerge until the question of minds as an extension of Mind came up – then she asked Matthew whether we were parts of his God in the way that Sarkar had just said that we were parts of Brahman, the Dwarf in the Middle and so on. Matthew said that he did not find the idea difficult, provided we didn't confuse the part with the whole – the Judaeo-Christian tradition stressed transcendence.

'So in that view we are all avatars?' said Cynthia.

'What do you mean by avatars?' said Matthew.

'Tell him, Sarkar,' I said.

'It means descents – descents of God into the persons of Man.'

'Some of them were only partial, weren't they?' said Cynthia.

'Oh, yes. Rama was a full avatara, Lakshmana only a partial avatara.'

'Rama's mother got more porridge?' said Cynthia.

'Yes, it is right. She knows the story,' said Sarkar. 'And Jesus Christ is a Christian avatara.'

'The only one,' said Malachi.

'Which is why you call him God's son,' said Sarkar.

'There is a linguistic point, isn't there?' I said. 'Doesn't "son of" in Hebrew imply "having the nature of" – like "sons of worthlessness"?'

'It does, David,' said Malachi.

'So if we and Jesus are brothers – sisters – we are also avatars?' said Cynthia. 'I think his point is that he is not unique.'

'Well,' said Matthew, 'that isn't the view of Tradition.'

'If Tradition got it right, why did Jesus tell us to pray to "our father" and not "my father"?' said Cynthia. For the rest of the session Matthew and Malachi were engaged – very creditably,

I thought, in a debate on psychopantheism. I think they learned a great deal. They might end up Quakers. I'd underestimated our Cynthia – it was a good point, and it opened up the subject.

Rabbit trouble: 'I say, David, are you quite sure you're teaching *philosophy*? From what I hear, it's a bit discursive, isn't it? I mean, quantum physics, radical politics, Christology .,.'

I imagine he'd been bugging my desk or pumping my students.

I said, 'Precisely – what do you think philosophy is?'

'Well, it's usually regarded as the development of a theory of knowledge, and it *has* a history ...'

'On which they get examined – right. But you don't think Socrates, Wittgenstein and Kant were delivering lectures in a syllabus, do you?'

'Well – er – no, but the students need to hear about them systematically ...'

'Which they do, and a lot else besides. Want to come and eavesdrop next week when we get going on moral and political philosophy? Better still, you give 'em an account of Rawls's theory of social justice – might be a good idea to vary the presenter? Are you on, Sir?'

From his face I reckoned he knew sweet Fanny Adams about the theory of justice – that one or any other – and would need two large carrots to get over the very idea. 'Oh, no – wouldn't dream of intruding into your class, David,' he said, 'just making a suggestion. When ideas are interesting it's awfully easy to lose the – er – curriculum backbone, isn't it? But you're doing a fine job – opening their minds – excellent course from that point of view – see you at the Staff Meeting,' and a mad dash back to his hutch.

Sharkey's card arrived when I'd just about despaired of hearing from him, and was beginning to think that the Satanic Mills of Spivsville had consumed him. It was a neat little expanded-type printout which said:

The Invisible Academy is convened at 7.00 pm on Thursday March 7 at this address. Swords and mental armour will be worn.

Handwritten underneath: 'Come round at six, David. I need to talk.'

The City hadn't effected any visible change in the Shark – he still looked a ruin, and I wondered if he went to Father's offices looking like that, and what Antrobus said behind his back.

'Something wrong, Shark?'

'Well, yes and no. First let me fill you in on what I am doing.'

'Running Father's information processing?'

'Oh yes, that – but I mean the real project, burrowing into Spivsville. You know, your Father's given me an incredible weapon: access to information. I knew it was powerful, but I simply didn't realise how powerful. *This* is the first part of the project.'

'This' was a fat computer printout headed, on the outer face, 'A GUIDE TO THE ESTABLISHMENT'.

'What I did,' said the Shark, 'what I did was simply to compile. We get the Stock Exchange dealings on-line. We can access share registers, on-line. We can get all the stuff in Whitaker, about who is who, on line. I took two hundred names as a starter – cabinet ministers, top civil service brass, some judges, the noisier tycoons plus some of the quieter ones, and some names out of the news. Just a sample for starters. I write a cross-search programme, and I leave it to run at night. Your old man has no idea of the cost of computer time, or he'd rent it out. In the morning's grey light I nip in and find a most instructive guide to everybody's racket? No such luck. Some of the fattest targets don't have an obvious racket, or they've got it under wraps. Back to the drawing board. First, get their wives' names from *Who's Who*: did you realise someone's put *Who's Who* on disc, at an advertising consultancy, and the entry to it was keyless because it was a public document and they didn't bother? Then, nominees: that was really tricky, because it's like breaking into a bank. I was going to try to hack some of them, but before I started I had a bright idea. I went round a lot of private bulletin boards. Would you believe it, some of the kids had hacked a nominee file and put the access route on a bulletin board and *nobody had spotted it*? I tapped the whole thing. Then I called the Bank and warned them about the bulletin board. They were bound to find out eventually, and I got Brownie points for public spirit. Of course, it's only one nominee company, but that's better than nothing. Now, that was the week of the Argotech takeover. Because I'd been monitoring in advance, I saw the turnup in prices two weeks ahead of the actual bid. I could send my tame demon back to check who held those shares. Then I hauled up the trawl.'

'Anything in it?'

'A lot of Spivsville sprats, and two big fat codfish. One's the wife of a Minister. The other has a daughter in the Monopolies Commission – that one's a Civil Service knight.'

'Insider dealing?'

'Insider bloody dealing. They've nearly all got the same broker, too. Very interesting.'

I told Sharkey he'd had a lot of fun, but the City watchdogs would be doing exactly the same, and even if they weren't, blowing up two fat cats wouldn't bring down the walls of Jericho. Moreover he'd get fired eventually for wasting computer time, the property of my father.

'You don't,' said Sharkey, 'send up rockets and start blowing people up. You remember Quintus Fabius, who bided his time, and you compile, and compile, and compile. One year from now, I should have a GUIDE TO THE ESTABLISHMENT which makes it possible to finger a lot of people.'

'If Father doesn't find out what you're at,' I said, 'and if the Courts haven't shut down the Press by then.'

'They won't, and he won't,' said Sharkey, 'and if he does, I can finger him – beside putting a virus into his computer which will bugger up his operations permanently. But that's the bad news, David. That's why you're here early.'

'Father's on the fiddle?' I said. 'Not surprising.'

'Only in a minor way, a bit of insider dealing, but it's small

55

and I doubt they could pin it on him. The real stumer is that Antrobus is ripping your father off. What's worse is that he's doing it in a way that will leave your old man with the baby. Mortgages – your father's backed them, Antrobus has got loans on them, and neither the properties nor the clients are at the addresses given. Your father's name is on all of them – Antrobus insisted that the chief partner had the privilege of signing. And the Company's legal officer is a character who was disbarred in 1979. Wonderful what you can get out of records. The point is, what do I do?'

'I would say, warn him in strict confidence. And write a confidential minute, keeping a copy. He'll have to clean it up.'

'Or sack me,' said Sharkey.

'That wouldn't be very clever,' I said, 'and we'll both see him. What's the scale of the operation?'

'Big.'

'I hope he can cover it.'

'If they go bust, I've lost my computer,' said Sharkey.

'And gained an imperishable reputation, Shark. You'll be rehired. By the bank you just warned that their files were leaking.'

'You cheer me up,' said Sharkey. 'Let's visit Father in short order.'

I could hear the others coming upstairs. Cynthia came in first, then Violet, then Dr Sarkar – evidently Sharkey had invited him. Violet was looking prosperous, a bit pink, either from the stairs, or because she was seeing me. I kissed her.

'You look fit,' I said. 'Have you found your niche?'

'Yes. Not what I expected, but it's my niche all right. I'm not teaching, I'm working for immigrants – in a legal service. That's your doing, David. I wouldn't have thought of it if I hadn't lived at your place. Thanks.'

'I'm glad it helped, Vi. All well otherwise?'

'Yes.'

'Getting laid regularly, I hope?'

'There are other things in my life. If I need that I'll know where it's available,' said Vi. Dr Sarkar looking a bit mystified, and wondering if he'd heard right.

56

'Right,' said Sharkey. 'We will begin. I'll report progress, and then we can take agenda items.'

'I've got one,' said Violet, putting her hand up. 'It's urgent, too.'

So Sharkey gave the same seminar he'd given me, leaving out Father.

'So,' said Sarkar, 'they are all in some degree compromisable.'

'Nice word,' said Sharkey. 'We hope so.'

'Now,' said Violet, 'it fits with my business – or I hope it does. Deportation – they've got a hundred and fifty people on a hulk off Harwich. One of them is a married man with two children. He had *time* to have two children before the palace eunuchs decided he only got married in order to stay here. His wife's threatening suicide. What do we do?'

'Stage a diversion and spring them?' I said. 'The guards on the hulk are from a commercial security firm – shouldn't be too hard if Mansur will lend me a few Sikhs.'

'Who,' said Sharkey, 'would we need to lean on?'

'Burnside, the Home Secretary. Up there,' said Violet, pointing to a large photograph of the Cabinet, sitting in rows. Sharkey used it as a dart board, with the PM scoring highest.

'They look like a Victorian representation of the ill-effects of self-abuse,' said Sharkey. 'Now, I didn't want to do this so soon, Vi, but Burnside is a match on my list. Insider dealing via his wife – she's bought twice now ahead of an announcement. It's not much to go on. I doubt if it's safe to use without something else.'

'Sharkey,' said Cynthia, 'this is difficult for me. Ethically, I mean. I do have the something else, but it was told me in professional confidence.'

'Counselling?' said Violet.

'Well, not quite. But we do try to keep strict confidence.'

'We?' said Sharkey.

'We. Specialist working girls,' said Cynthia, sweetly. 'Don't any of you pretend you didn't guess.'

'Hadn't the remotest idea,' said Sharkey.

Sarkar looked puzzled and was about to ask a question.

57

'I'll explain after,' I hissed.

'Go on, Cynth. Don't say he's one of yours,' said Sharkey.

'He is not one of mine. I wouldn't work on Westminster,' said Cynthia, 'they're kinky and dangerous, a lot of them – but there are girls who do.'

'You exchange professional confidences?' said Sharkey. 'Oh, boy!'

'They're chiefly warnings. We need to know which of them give you bruises.'

'And Burnside sahib gives girls bruises?' said Vi.

'No, he's fairly harmless. He likes suspender belts,' said Cynthia.

'Well, I like suspender belts,' said Sharkey.

'You don't want to wear them, though – or perhaps you do: sorry if I sounded critical,' said Cynthia.

'I don't. But do you know the lady's name?'

'Yes. That's the point.'

'And I know the Swiss broker who tips him off,' said Sharkey. 'Snap.'

'Enough to go on, Shark?' I said.

'It might well be. I didn't want a trial run so soon. But Vi's client needs the College's assistance. What's his name, Vi?'

'Mr V.P. Wikramasinghe.'

'He is a Tamil?' said Sarkar.

'Yes.'

'Right,' said Sharkey. 'Proposal one. We write a very innocent letter on his behalf. We send it to the Home Secretary's private address. What's the lady's name?'

'Mari Beauchamp.'

'Good. We simply say that our request has the support of Ms Mari Beauchamp and of Herr Erlenmeyer of Zurich, and a Press conference in support of Mr Earwig's application will be held shortly. David and I will draft it.'

'And we all sign it?' said Sarkar, hopefully.

'Don't be bloody daft,' said Sharkey. 'We sign it John Bull or something. If we do this a few times that's going to become a name of terror.'

I wasn't surprised about Cynthia's occupation, because I

knew. A few days before I'd gone round to her address with a class paper. I noticed two windows upstairs were covered in black cardboard – a photographic darkroom, no doubt. There was a small, folded note pinned to her door, labelled 'WALTER'. I'm not Walter, neither am I handicapped by scruples. It read:

Your Mistress is occupied and will have no need of you until six p.m. Thursday. In the meantime you will wear the costume assigned to you and perform the tasks I gave you. If you fail in any particular, you will be disciplined unmercifully. Dominatrix.

Well, well, well. Knowing Cynthia a little, the charade must be bloody hard work. But she'd be equal to it if she felt she was helping somebody, siphoning off problems, acting as a lightning conductor for Spivsville. Kind, public-spirited Cynthia.

'David?' she said, after the meeting.

'Nice work, Cynthia.'

'Yes. Listen, David. I've got a friend who's a sensitive. If we applied ourselves, do you think …'

'We could pinpoint some fields for Sharkey to work on, using ESP?' I said.

'You don't discount it?'

'No, the military don't. But isn't it far too erratic?'

'Not,' said Cynthia, 'if you see remote pictures, as my friend does.'

'I thought remote viewing referred to pictures being deliberately transmitted by a group,' I said. 'I'd rather have a bug in the Cabinet Office.'

'Well,' said Cynthia, 'we can *try*.'

I walked her to the evening class, and left one of the physicists – the one we called Gonzo – explaining to her that the Einstein-Podolsky paradox and Aspect's experiment didn't mean that particles can communicate by ESP.

I needed a lot of support from Sharkey to make our visit to Father. From the fact that we arrived unannounced, and together, he must have realised something was up. We went

59

straight into his office like business visitors, no greetings, no sherry.

Sharkey opened his case, got out the printouts, and delivered his seminar.

Father said, 'Is this true?'

I suggested that if it hadn't been we wouldn't be there telling it to him.

'Mr Sharkey shouldn't have involved you. He should have come straight to me. You're supposed to be a confidential employee, Sharkey. I don't like this – don't like it at all.'

I pointed out that since the family honour looked like going down the tubes, Sharkey had shown considerable sensitivity in asking me what to do: I was his son, after all, and if he was going in the slammer I'd at least like some advance notice. Father ignored that. He said, 'All of the mortgages?'

'Well, a very substantial proportion, Sir – of those I've checked so far.'

'I'd better,' said Father, 'call Antrobus.'

'You'd better not,' I said, 'because if he gets a breath of this he'll be in Antofagasta before you can say Dartmoor. What you had better do is call your solicitor before anyone else stumbles on this. You've been set up, Father. If you don't get in first you're in bad trouble – like conspiracy to commit fraud.'

Well, he did call his solicitor. We had an awkward hour, with Mother looking round the door at intervals, while he came over. When he did come, he listened, and promptly called the Fraud Squad, pointing out that if Father himself exposed the scam he might get away with negligence, but if he didn't he was for the high jump, so Mother served lunch – charming to everyone and not a single question as to what the flap was about – and we waited for the heavies to arrive. Father and the Shark made the statements the solicitor had told them to make. Then the squad took the printouts with them and went to find Antrobus.

'I have to warn you,' said the solicitor, 'that we're not out of the wood yet, not by any means. I think it's only reasonable to assume that Mr Antrobus will put the blame on you, and

60

there is a risk that he's prepared evidence for the purpose. Don't talk to him if he calls, don't make any statements to anybody, and let me know at once if you get any Press enquiries. In that case, it would be advisable for you to stay at my flat rather than here.'

And leave mother to be very nice to them, give them tea, and tell them she knew absolutely nothing about it. Yes, she knew Mr Antrobus. No, she didn't know he'd just been nicked for fraud – how very sad! She was sure it would all be cleared up in the end. I could just hear it.

Father didn't even thank Sharkey, but he did say, 'I hope you realise that I'm extremely grateful, David. You handled a ghastly situation very well. Probably glad you didn't join us, because so far as I can see we're out of business.' I was about to say that if Master Antrobus talked his way out of this one I'd get the bugger for him, but it wasn't the time.

'Anything I can do to help, Father?'

'I don't think so, David. You could come back and see us before too long.'

I said I would, and we left. Mother was beginning to flutter. Father went back inside, to start explaining.

'Well, I'm bloody sorry for the old chap,' said Sharkey. 'He's been taken for a terrific ride by this Antrobus fellow. Simply didn't know what was going on in his own outfit – if he's speaking the truth. You do understand, David, I didn't plan this – for once I'm actually doing what he's paying me for.'

I told Sharkey I was thankful it was he who had rumbled the scam and not some outside auditor, because there was at least a chance of damage control, and the firm had caught up with Antrobus itself, so Father might be able to salvage something.

'Glad you see it that way,' said Shark. 'Come back to my place, if you aren't too knackered – we've got a letter to write, remember?'

It ran:

Dear Minister,

We thought it proper to approach you personally. We are

61

interested in the case of Mr V.P. Wikramasinghe, who is now awaiting deportation, and who has a wife and two children legally resident in this country.

We shall be pressing the proper authorities to obtain testimony germane to this case from Ms Mari Beauchamp, and from Herr Max Erlenmeyer of Helvetia Associated Brokers. We shall be making a statement to the Press on the subject next Thursday – unless of course Mr Wikramasinghe's appeal has been heard by that time, and the matter of additional evidence has become moot.

I am, Sir, etc.
JOHN LILBURN

There was a nice, computer-printed letterhead reading 'INSTITUTE OF PERSONAL INFORMATION STUDIES', and a logo, collaged and xeroxed on, which showed a Greek Fury with a torch, surrounded by the inscription 'raro antecedentem scelestum deseruit pede Poena claudo'.

'It'll be wasted on Burnside,' I said.

'It won't,' said Sharkey. 'He was a lecturer in Classics.'

'Bet you he won't know who Honest John Lilburn was.'

'He'll be too shitless to care, I hope,' said Sharkey. 'Now, put on these gloves, take a fresh sheet, xerox it and sign it. Now the envelope – address it by hand. Take it out of the middle of the packet. Don't lick it, you cretin – they type saliva these days. Now, put it in this bag. We can tip it into the post without touching it. Bingo!' He laid it religiously by. 'I say, David,' he said, 'your old man isn't a crook, is he?'

'No. He's got pin-joints in his conscience, but he's not a crook,' I said.

Sharkey became unusually communicative after the letter was posted. I was interested to know where he had got his ideas – were they the result of his peculiar brain architecture?

'My role model,' said Sharkey, and he gave me a seminar on Hamsen. To the Shark, Hamsen was a semidivine character, one of Sarkar's avataras. He had been picked up at sixteen by Turing and given all kinds of technician's assignments in order to keep him around, during the days when digital computation was being invented. Given his own research project, he'd upset his bosses by refusing to discuss it with certain bigwigs of the atomic programme, notably Klaus Fuchs: for this he absolutely refused to give a reason. When Fuchs was arrested, Security came down on Hamsen like a ton of bricks. Did he know Fuchs was passing information to the Russians? 'Oh, yes,' said Hamsen – he'd conducted his own enquiries. Then why didn't he say so? 'I didn't,' said Hamsen, 'want to interfere with what he was doing. I think he's probably prevented the Americans from starting World War Three.' They didn't like that at all. If Hamsen felt like that, why did he refuse to talk to him, or have him involved in his work? 'Because,' said Hamsen, 'in discussing artificial intelligence, it's impossible to work with people who have hidden agendas. It affects their actual scientific work. To work on AI you must be wholly transparent.' They said, 'Thou wast altogether conceived in sin, and dost thou teach us?' and they cast him out, into the university circuit, where at the end of his career he met Sharkey, the old magician and the young magician. Hamsen, said Sharkey, taught him all he knew.

'Is he around?' I asked.

'Retired.' I think Sharkey considered him immortal. 'It sounds as if we could use him,' I suggested.

Sharkey smoothed down his abominable pullover. 'Either he could destroy Spivsville single-handed,' he said, 'or he's the one person who'd spot what we were at, and stop us. I don't know which he would do. He wouldn't care for Spivsville, and he owes them for what they did to Turing. But he might think we weren't lucid. What I've got in mind might possibly offend him – there's absolutely no way of knowing.'

'He seems to have respected you,' I said.

'Magicians,' said Sharkey, 'train sorcerer's apprentices, but if they see them making what they conceive to be dangerous uses of magic they intervene. Hamsen will relish what I've got in mind after I've done it – I don't think I could tell him I meant to do it. Frustrating me would be too big a temptation.'

'You think someone might call him in when things begin to happen?'

'It's my waking nightmare. But if he did come back, I would

know. If we start to be countered. His counterprogramming has his signature on it.'

'There must be other bright guys,' I said.

Sharkey shook his head. 'I've got Hamsen's magic. I'm the only student who stuck to him like a leech until I'd got it all. If I'm countered, that will be Hamsen – and Hamsen will know whom he's countering. We know one another's programming styles, we *share* a style – it's like knowing one another's voices. Or a radio operator's fist.' Sharkey didn't mention Hamsen again. But watching him when he had one of his cloudcapped periods I knew, from then on, with whom he was communing.

7

Some good seemed to have come out of the Winslow riot: when yobs disrupted the local Caribbean carnival, the police dealt with the whole thing sensibly – no inoffensive citizens beaten up, and all the characters who were arrested were by local repute villains. Oggie would have approved; Mansur, and even Winston, had a good word for the Force.

At the class, Cynthia came in looking like a cat who had eaten the canary. She came straight to the desk where I was getting out books.

'Mr Wikramasinghe's been sent home, pending a court hearing. Vi just called me,' she said.

'Sounds as if it worked,' I muttered, 'but mum's the word.' It might, of course, have nothing to do with John Lilburn and Sharkey. But if it had, this was going to be habit-forming.

'Vi told me to say – now what about the other hundred and fifty?' said Cynthia, and retired to her place.

When we dismissed, I went down to the cafeteria. Father Malachi had got there before me – he was drinking coffee and looking under the weather. I was surprised to see him on his own – he and Matthew hunted in pairs as a rule.

'Mind if I join you?' I said.

'Not at all, David – sit down.'

'You look knackered: had a heavy day?' I said.

Malachi grinned ruefully, 'It shows, does it?'

'I'm afraid the course is a bit exhausting – virtue goes out of one talking.'

'With me,' said Malachi 'it's the flood of ideas.'

'You're having to listen to an awful lot of heresy, Rev.'

'I haven't heard any heresy,' said Malachi. 'What I have been hearing is a mass of concepts I simply haven't met before. We were brought up on Aquinas and Abelard, not quantum logics.'

'Tough,' I said, 'if you've got a professional position.'

'I have a commitment, of course. I'm a priest,' said Malachi.

I said that so far as I could see ideas like the virtual character of reality didn't really impinge much on any of the theistic religions. Christ never lectured on the nature of the universe: Cardinal Bellarmine and the Fundamentalists who didn't like Darwin had got their categories mixed. The only thing we had said which might be doctrinally off limits was the idea that minds might be continuous with Mind. 'Teilhard thought so, and he was a good Catholic – probably a better Catholic than philosopher: he's inclined to get airborne.'

'It's not a problem of doctrine,' said Malachi, 'it's a problem of reconciliation. I simply hadn't seen these possibilities before.'

'Do they need reconciling?' I asked him.

'For me they do. I have a mind,' said Malachi.

'Are you bothered that the Tradition doesn't include them?'

'Not really – yet I find they have been around for centuries and the Church hasn't looked at them properly.'

'If it bothers you that the Church burned Giordano Bruno and booted out Meister Eckhard, just remember we're all sinners,' I said. 'Theologians are actually more open and tolerant now than scientists.'

'I hope you don't think I'm occupationally inflexible' said Malachi. 'Non-Catholics get it very wrong, you know. I'm not obligated to agree with the Church, only to observe its magisterium as a matter of discipline.'

I told him I thought I did understand what he was saying – though not, of course, the emotional experience of being a Catholic and a priest. 'If you're a soldier, you may have your own views on square-bashing, but you do it because you value regimental tradition and the concept of obeying orders without question. It's a perfectly reasonable position.'

'Added to that,' said Malachi, 'my regimental loyalty as you call it, can you conceive the responsibility of being empowered to say Mass and consecrate the Elements?'

'I can conceive it,' I said, 'because for me, everything one does is sacramental. If it isn't, it's merely trivial and one shouldn't be doing it.'

Malachi thought for a long time. 'It must be difficult to live with that belief, David – if every meal was sacramental. The Real Presence would be disabling.'

'Well,' I said, 'the Jews wear yarmulkchs to remind them that they are constantly in the presence of the Absolute. What I think is lacking in me is a sense of awe – it comes back to what we were saying: you can't be in awe of something of which you are a part.'

'Are you yourself a Buddhist, David?' said Malachi.

I told him I wasn't an 'ist' of any kind: some Buddhist ideas seemed to me to chime with science and to provide a better backdrop than hardhat positivism, but that was provisional: the only dogma I had was that dogmata had to be provisional, because if they weren't one couldn't learn.

'It would be difficult,' said Malachi, 'to be your own teacher, and not fall into error.'

'Well, it's a risk, but the Tradition can be equally wrong.'

'So can your mother,' said Malachi, 'but one can't dispense with parents.'

I asked him if he ever talked to his confessor about the philosophy class.

'He's most helpful,' said Malachi. 'He says that it will strengthen my awareness of discipline, and I agree with him.'

'But it's a bit of a battle,' I said.

'It's a necessary battle. Your classes are making me a better priest,' said Malachi, 'able to distinguish the essential from the non-essential.'

He'd stopped looked knackered, I thought. It probably did him more good to talk to me than to Fr Matthew, who was probably digesting too.

'About the superposition of lives,' said Malachi, 'reincarnation was declared a heresy by the Councils of 1274 and

1439, but they slipped in the doctrine of Purgatory: God might choose to perfect the imperfect, but they forbade speculation concerning how and where. I don't think the Councils would have known what a coherent superposition was.' And he finished his coffee with relish.

Letter – something wholly unprecedented – from Father. He wanted to see me – equally unprecedented – at his office, where Mother wouldn't be around to ask questions, I assumed. I only found out later that he was still staying away from home for fear of the Press. His lawyer had persuaded him to let it be known that he had gone to New York. There he was, holed up in the office, probably with false whiskers, or in drag, but there hadn't been a word in the Press – nothing about him, nothing about Antrobus, silence.

I was digesting this when Mansur stuck his head in.

'There is a young woman walking up and down looking at the house.'

'So?'

'No doubt she is looking for you,' said Mansur.

The Violet business had given Mansur an odd idea of my private life, but it wasn't worth trying to disabuse him. I looked out. It was Sarah. I wondered why she didn't come in – she knew exactly where I lived. I opened the window and whistled.

'You see,' said Mansur, and went.

'Why didn't you come in?' I asked her, taking a very smart coat.

'I wasn't sure – I didn't want to upset Violet.'

'Don't be a chump, Sarah – Violet liked you.'

'Liked?' said Sarah.

'She's not here now, if that's what you mean.'

'I thought you were more or less permanent,' said Sarah.

'On and off – she got a vocation and needed to do her thing elsewhere,' I said.

I couldn't help wondering if Sarah had come to see if there were any vacancies, but she hadn't – it was an extension of the affaire Antrobus. She wanted me to know that she had suspected something, but she had never been able to get any evidence apart from feminine intuition about Antrobus and – this was the punch line – she hadn't let Father down.

'I didn't think you had,' I said. '*He* let *you* down.'

'That,' said Sarah, 'but I just didn't want you to think I'd conspired against him. Or blown the whistle on him to get even. You told me to blackmail him, you know. Since somebody's obviously talked, I wanted to tell you it wasn't me: I loved him, which was stupid of me, wasn't it?'

I said I didn't think it was stupid: I imagined he could be very pathetic and vulnerable and hence attractive in a way.

'But,' I said, 'how did you know there was trouble? It hasn't been in the papers. The shit will hit the fan any moment, but it hasn't done so yet.'

'I heard at work,' said Sarah. 'I'm working for the new Stock Exchange Regulatory Commission.'

'Holy cow!' I said. 'Do they know you worked for Father?'

'They know I worked for him,' said Sarah, with the emphasis on 'worked'. 'My boss asked me if I thought the firm was clean, and I told him I had no reason to think otherwise, and he left it at that. But the funny thing is the way a sort of lid has come down: I thought they might be keeping it from me, but nobody's heard any more. It's simply been taken off the files.'

'Probably Antrobus plays tiddleywinks with the Prime Minister,' I said.

'Very funny, but I think it really is something like that. I think that nasty creature is going to get away with it.'

'Or dump it on Father?'

'No, because if he was going to do that, the case would have to go ahead. It's just disappeared.'

'Well,' I said, 'I'm glad you told me. I'm not sure whether I ought to be pleased or not.'

Sarah was very serious, very decorative and smelt very nice. It struck me that Father had actually offered me a rather gauche birthday present and I'd been a bit churlish about it because of the circumstances, but this wasn't the moment and it was going to need thinking about. Also

Sharkey would pounce, if he knew, and say we now had a pipeline into the Regulatory Commission. It was bad enough Sarah being exploited by one generation, let alone by two – though I thought she had done a lot of growing since she left Father, and was quite able to look after herself. I'd leave it to her to cue me, and see how things developed. She didn't cue me, so I shook hands, pecked her on the cheek, and hoped she'd come again.

'And I hope Violet comes back, when she's finished what she has to do,' said Sarah.

'That,' I said, 'is up to her. We're good friends.'

I called Sharkey and told him the word was that Spivsville was closing ranks. 'I know,' said Sharkey. 'Great!'

'Why great?'

'Because if the word came from on high, it won't just be Antrobus we can blow up. Incidentally, David, I wouldn't use this phone. It's clean at the moment, but it's not good practice.'

I remember going to Father's office as a child. They gave me a pile of paper slips out of the waste basket, and I had a delightful time making banknotes out of them with rubber stamps and a red ink-pad. The room was dusty and brown, like a station waiting room, and there were tall wooden cabinets. The bricks in the passage were painted brown, and white near the ceiling. The bricks in the washroom had shiny tile surfaces. There were huge washbasins, and I had to be held up to piss in the urinals which had a tank over them that gurgled. I hadn't been back once since. Not even the address was the same.

Now it was all glass – glass doors, glass walls, a glass atrium roof, glass elevators, *Ficus* and *Monstera* in little internal beds of peat, fake plants where it was too dark to grow real ones, the Crystal Cathedral on Mars – if you went outside you'd asphyxiate for lack of air, but nobody wanted to go outside. Why should they? They had their little glass offices looking out on the plants they'd captured – they had matching receptionists – pussies on wheels with look-alike smiles doing

70

their nails at designer desks and wearing headsets and little microphones on stalks, and presiding over little pots with tropical plants in them: Father's ant-nest. The ants were scurrying up and down the escalators carrying papers as if they'd chewed them from a tree, but both streams were loaded. Ants usually show you where they are at work. One stream is loaded, the other carrying nothing. Occasionally they touch antennae or pass over a drop of plant juice. These didn't. I lost my way and got into a room full of VDUs and shouting, rather like a noisy newsroom. The voices I remember from childhood were boss-class, modulated. These were Croynge. You could hear the commission-hunting edge on them. The powerhouse of good old Spivsville in full cry, as busy as a toolshop and a lot less matey, but there were no trucks of parts going out, no metal stock coming in. I'd seen it before – the toolshop analogy was false: this was the fruit-machine room in Caesar's Palace without the flashing lights. I watched them making commissions or mistakes, the only things actually made here, until a pussy-on-wheels from the clone asked if she could help me, Sir? She took me one level up, to Father.

He was behind several sets of doors and a bevy of the clonal sisters, and to get to him we went through a sort of chapel with large chairs arranged round a table and an episcopal throne (Father's?) at the end. Beside the clonal sisters he had two goons in blue uniforms, each with his portrait on a badge – obviously the office knew father was here, even if the press thought he was in New York. I didn't have a badge, but apparently they'd been briefed.

'David!' said Father. The damned office was straight out of *Dallas*. 'I wanted you to hear the good news. And I wanted you to meet somebody.'

'Don't tell me – Antrobus has got religion, confessed all, and returned the swag.'

'Nothing like that,' said Father, 'but we are in the clear.'

'How could you be?' I said. 'I thought you got me here to tell me you were off to Venezuela.'

He looked pained. 'We had some anxious moments,' he said.

71

A thing on his desk buzzed and said that Mister Gorringe was here. 'Good, send him in,' said Father.

'He's here to explain?' I said.

'Yes. I wanted your mind put at rest. You understand that, I hope. I don't want my son to – er –'

'Think you're on the fiddle? I didn't think that,' I said. 'Antrobus took you for a ride. *I* didn't think you were a crook.'

Gorringe: a rather varnished young man who smelt of Parliamentary candidate (cheap soap, incense, aftershave, sales course) and shook hands insincerely at arms' length.

'Oh, Gorringe: glad you could come. This is my son.'

'And you're what? Fraud squad?' I said.

'No, no,' waxy grin, 'Cabinet Office.'

I might have guessed it: letting Father drown was going to be one too many for somebody, so they'd thrown him a life-belt.

'I wanted you to explain what has happened,' said Father. 'I thought David should know – in confidence, of course, David.'

'Of course!'

'It was he who came to see me with our computer expert, Mr Sharkey. We owe him an explanation.'

'Well!' said Gorringe. 'You'll be pleased to hear that everything's been sorted out.'

'And Antrobus has been dropped in the Thames in a cement overcoat?' I said.

No sense of humour. 'Mr Antrobus, and your father, were in fact the victims of a client. No blame attaches to anyone in this firm. The Police have established that. I thought you'd be relieved,' said Gorringe.

'Who was the client?' I said.

'Well,' said Gorringe, 'that's really confidential, I'm afraid.'

'Don't tell me. He was an Iranian arms dealer who was wished on you by the CIA.'

'No comment, of course,' said Gorringe, 'but he was an – er – foreigner.' He grinned unhappily.

'Selling dud mortgages in England?'

'Er – yes.'

'So you've nicked him?' I asked. 'It hasn't made the Press.'

'We've talked to him. There are problems about prosecution.

And it won't make the Press,' said Gorringe. 'That's what we – er – wanted to say to you. What I'm telling you must remain strictly confidential – you do understand that, I'm sure. Business confidence is very easily damaged. Your Father could be seriously hurt by any publicity.'

'I take it, then, that you've got the money back?' I said.

'All the mortgages have been satisfactorily covered.'

'Covered?'

'By the City. They've assumed them, to end your Father's exposure.'

'And Antrobus, who was the victim of the fraud, felt he had to resign,' said Father. 'I asked him to remain, but he didn't feel able to do so.'

'In other words, on top of loot, you paid him off.'

'Certainly not – he's entitled to severance, of course.'

'Of course. I take it that what has actually happened is that the taxpayer picked up the tab.' They both looked pained.

'You entirely misunderstand …' Gorringe began.

'If not,' I said, 'what's the Cabinet Office doing here?'

'The Government,' said Gorringe, 'is deeply concerned with London's good name as an international business centre. I would have thought that was obvious. And if I may say so, you ought to be pleased this embarrassing business has been resolved without financial loss to your Father. You do seem rather cynical about it.'

'Don't mind me, I'm a philosopher,' I said. 'Of course I'm delighted, for both my parents' sake. And I won't blow any whistles – I can't very well, can I?'

'No,' said Gorringe. 'I'm delighted you see it that way.'

'I take it,' I said, 'that you've fired Sharkey?'

'Certainly not,' said Father. 'A most able young man. It was his sharpness that saved our bacon. I tremble to think what would have happened if you and he hadn't warned me. I owe you both a very great deal, David.'

It would have been daft to go and find Sharkey at the office, and I didn't try. When I did see him, in his flat, he was not indignant but cock-a-hoop – he'd followed the whole cover-up from his console.

'They told me the same tale,' said Sharkey. 'Now you,

David, would have said "Don't play silly buggers with me." I took it like a lamb. They've raised my salary ten G's. And this' – he pointed to his establishment file – 'is pure gold. Of course the Treasury paid. It was a Cabinet decision. Ostensibly it's to save the good name of the City – actually at least two Ministers were mixed up in the Iranian consortium which pulled the scam. They didn't know about it, but it would have looked pretty bad.'

'I said it was Iranian – they must think I knew,' I said.

'Teach you to keep your mouth shut when you make a good guess,' said Sharkey. 'You thought we'd never get enough explosive to threaten the system. Well, you were wrong.'

'If you set it off, we'll blow up my Father,' I said.

'No ethical problem,' said Sharkey. 'I won't set it off. Not prematurely. I don't want to sink two ministers – this gang could ride that out. Remember Quintus Fabius, David.'

8

Cynthia missed the next class – she was away covering the Party Conferences. Sharkey had apparently overcome her reluctance to associate with politicians, in the public interest. Fr Matthew said he never realised that Cynthia was into politics.

Fr Malachi buttonholed me outside. 'David, now you've finished indoctrinating me, it's my turn to indoctrinate you. Come and learn the facts of life.'

I told him I thought I knew them. 'Not those facts,' said Malachi. 'Will you get yourself in here?'

Here was a rather dilapidated shooting brake, with what appeared to be a dead body propped into a sitting posture and wrapped in blankets in the back.

'What the hell's that, Malachi?'

'It's soup. Double duty – the blankets kept it hot while you were discoursing, and it warms the blankets.'

'Where are we going for our lesson?'

'It's the freeway arches tonight,' said Malachi. 'Sure to be a good congregation.'

And there was. All the arches tall enough to be useful had doors and were let out for storage. Malachi stopped the wagon among puddles and rubbish, with the traffic bellowing past at head level and the ground shaking. The tallest arch here was about four feet and pitch dark, but Malachi had an enormous torch, which he shone considerately at the roof – 'Mustn't dazzle people' – and ducked inside with me after him. He knocked on a cardboard box, and a head came out. The place smelt of sewer and public school. 'Don't come out, I'll bring it,' said Malachi. 'David, go back and start filling. There's plastic cups in the bag. Take the blankets off and you'll feel the tap. And chuck me in the sliced bread. Mister Willie, you still here? Emma! Are you at home? Eight cups here, David.' He came out, and the two of us started a bucket chain. It fed into the the dark hole, into hands, disappeared. Eight mugs, then the patched-up blankets. 'No, you don't return them,' Malachi yelled over the hellish thunder inside the hole, 'but if you don't take them with you, fold them and leave them. Yes, take them with you if you're coming back or they'll fly away.' He was out of sight in the hole. 'Yes, of course I will.' Muttering – Malachi officiating, I thought – if it was a confession that diabolical booming ensured privacy. He came out, shaking a few hands – no faces, only the boxes; I could see them shaking, as if we were in the eye of a bombardment. In the next, still lower arch, there were faces – Eisenstein faces, Gorky faces. 'Ten mugs here, David – there's another sliced loaf.' A woman's face, old, tidy, rather sweet. Malachi was having his coat plucked. Miraculously for about three seconds the traffic shut down, though boo-oom went on in the depths of the hole: about two foot six high, this one. The woman had a soft Scots voice. She said, 'I think he's deid.'

Malachi was kneeling over somebody, doing his thing, giving the body its ticket. Suddenly figures carrying their disposable plastic cups, dragging boxes, irregular-shaped people with burdens, scattered out of the hole. One shouted into the next hole: more figures, more scurrying. They disappeared like a shower of leaves. Malachi came out.

'They'll get no sleep here tonight,' he said. 'We'll have to notify him, and they'll not want to answer questions. That's a disaster – it's starting to rain, too.'

'You know them?' I asked.

'The regulars, yes. They organise the others, the ones who've only just become homeless.'

'Who are the non-regulars?'

'All kinds – looking for work, youngsters kicked out of board and lodging, discharged patients. The old hands look after

76

them pretty well. It's cleaner here than the Spike, and less dangerous.'

'That hellish noise. It's like living inside a huge bell.'

'That,' said Malachi, 'is the voice of our delightful society. Sister Agnes!'

There were two figures picking their way to the wagon. A nun, and a Salvationist in a peaked cap, carrying a hamper between them.

'Too late,' yelled Malachi, 'there's been a death here and they've scattered. Try Milsom Street! MILSOM STREET!'

'Let's give them a ride,' I said.

'It's quicker through the pedestrian tunnel, and they may find some of ours kipping down there. Lucky we got here before they spotted this poor chap – at least they got their stores. We have to find a phone box next.'

Two streets away, driving through a gentrified yuppidom. Lit streets, estate agents, a few kerb-crawling cars looking for girls.

'Tell me, David,' said Malachi, 'do you believe in the reality of evil?'

I told him I'd think about that one. I certainly believed in the denaturing effect of greed, sanctimoniousness and emotional atrophy. One could get distorted enough to drop out of the human race altogether.

'I didn't think,' said Malachi, 'that Buddhists *did* believe in evil.'

'Maybe not – they say it's difficult enough to attain human form and not lose it. And I'm not a paid-up Buddhist, as I've already told you, Rev,' I said. 'I might not make the grade. You want to help those folk piecemeal, and good luck to you – I want to get even with the people responsible and put back a decent Britain.'

'It's a point of difference,' said Malachi. 'At this point one traditionally says one wants to touch the hearts of the dropouts from human decency. Then I think whose hearts I'm supposed to be touching. It would be simpler to touch them with a .303, but that would be a breach of orders.'

'Liberation theology stirring in you, Rev?' I said.

77

'If it didn't I'd deserve to be clobbered myself,' said Malachi.

'You know,' said Malachi, 'there was a bastard of a dictator in South America called Manuel dos Santos. The chap was a bloody monster who impaled people. He used to confess regularly to his chaplain. Well, the chaplain had had about enough, and after one particularly beastly atrocity, he decided to refuse dos Santos absolution. Dos Santos ordered him to give it, and when he wouldn't, had him whipped to death, and sent for another young priest. Well, Priest no. 2 looked over his orders for guidance, did some praying, and agreed. He heard dos Santos's confession, absolved him, laid one hand on his head and blessed him, and with the other hand he cut his throat. The Church talked quite seriously about canonising Priest no. 1 – after all, he was a fully paid-up martyr. The locals unofficially canonised them both and still give them a joint saints' day. It occurs to me that maybe there is a lesson there somewhere, don't you think, David? Join me tomorrow – I'll be doing some of the Prime Minister's bed and breakfast hotels.'

The Party Conferences on television: first we watched the Cheese and Wine Party sabotaging the Liberals ('You can almost see the nuclear strings stretching all the way to Langley, Va.' said the Shark) then the Leader of the Opposition doing an eloquent Welsh job, holding off *his* saboteurs with one hand and the Infantile Leftists with the other: and finally the Occupying Power in full cry – cocky, spiteful, and disgusting even to some of its own moderates. The one-party state on its triumphant way, with about the same majority as put Hitler in office.

'What does one do, Sharkey?' I asked, 'apart from simply throwing up, or emigrating?'

'One keeps one's head and waits,' said Sharkey, 'while staying hopping mad – it's a healthy emotion, and I commend it to you.'

As for Violet, she was in perpetual motion all through the coronation of the Witch of Endor.

'Longing to have a go, aren't you?'

'Well, aren't you? Father Malachi, how many candles would I have to light to let someone sneak a Claymore mine through security?'

'Well, Our Lord cast out the moneychangers, but he didn't reduce them to sausage meat,' said Malachi. 'Hatred is a pretty exhausting emotion. Come and lend a hand with my homeless folk if you can't be aisy, Violet.'

'Bandaid,' said Violet. 'Look at them sitting smirking – like ducks in a shooting gallery. But there's too much security.'

'Well, actually, there isn't,' said Sharkey, 'there's never enough security to defeat an intelligent adversary – if that's the appropriate way to go.'

'Then,' said Violet, 'why are we sitting here?'

'Because,' said Sharkey, 'at this point it's not the intelligent way to go. It's also much too late to set up anything this time if it were appropriate. Concentrate on something sensible, and keep on plugging away – which is what I'm doing.'

Violet opined that the Shark had a big mouth, but she'd put more faith in someone who was willing to take risks. Sharkey grinned and promised to visit her in jail. I think he was a bit worried about Violet, and blamed me for wishing her on the Disciples. After she had flounced out, Malachi told him not to worry.

'I do worry. If she cuts off Malcchus' ear, I don't have the spiritual wherewithal to stick it back on,' said Sharkey. 'That woman would miss her target, maim some inoffensive Parliamentary wives, get herself arrested, and provide a further excuse for a police state.'

Sharkey's next report to the group was euphoric: he was quietly chasing the fringes of the Antrobus affair in every direction, telling us it was creeping nearer to Downing Street. He distributed floppy discs like large communion wafers to all the disciples. 'Stow them away, put them in bank deposit boxes, hide them in books,' he ordered. 'All the dirt has to be multiplexed in case they get onto us.'

I raised the question of Malachi – should we try to edge him into the group? Sharkey said he didn't trust priests, let alone cadet Jesuits. Violet put up her hand.

'Whether he joins us or not, I want him.'

'What for, Vi?' I said.

'We're going after the other hundred and fifty. We're going to spring them.'

'Not from the group, Vi,' said Sharkey. 'I don't care what you do, but this group doesn't raise its profile. It would only take one of us being caught at some caper to focus attention on us. I forbid it.'

'It's not a group operation and you can't forbid it, Shark. It's my operation and my underground railroad – OK?'

Sharkey shrugged and said he didn't like it. I said that I wanted in.

'Sorry, David – no. Not you. You'd play soldiers,' said Vi. I pointed out that I'd suggested it. Vi shook her head.

'But you can get me that priest, if you think he'd help.'

'Well, at least he'd keep quiet about it if I ask him. What do you want him for?'

'A priest could get onto that prison ship. Somebody has to act as courier, otherwise they won't know what to do when we move.'

'I'll sound him,' I said. 'Shark, I suppose you don't object to some staff work in the group? Vi will need backup. Mind telling us what the plan is, Vi?'

'We were thinking of a diversion – making the security men an offer they can't refuse. We'll need to get all the refugees in one place – a religious service would be great,' said Vi. 'We need to have them on the car deck – it's near the side cargo hatch. I've got photographs.' She spread them out.

'One hundred and fifty Hindus going to hear Mass?' said Sarkar.

'They can make it a puja.'

'What sort of diversion had you in mind?' said Sharkey.

'We thought smoke – and pyrotechnics. A big fire on a barge alongside. Either we'll happen to be there and help to evacuate the ship, or we'll evacuate it while the screws are busy. If we wait until it's foggy we can thicken that with some more smoke – can you make us some, Dr Sarkar?'

'Oh yes, titanium oxide, but it is cheaper to buy smoke bombs in America,' said Sarkar. 'For flames we spill some naphtha – it can't set fire to the ship.'

'I suppose you're set on doing it the hard way,' said Sharkey. 'In a few weeks I may be able to put more heat on the Home Secretary.'

'In a few weeks they may get sent back,' said Vi, 'and if not, how would you like a few more weeks on a hulk, scared stiff you'd be sent back?'

'It wants split-second planning, Vi. You want the smoke on the windward side. There's only one anchor chain, so she'll swing with the tide.'

'We've thought of that.'

'Boats?'

'We've got four organised. It'll be a crush, but they'll float. And we're renting police uniforms for the *Pirates of Penzance* – we've said it's modern dress. Only takes a few. And we've got a furniture van. Any other questions?'

'Yes,' I said, 'why am I out?'

'Because you'd try to take command. Sorry, David – you showed me the Colonel sahib, remember? We don't need a ninja – somebody will get hurt. Our group has Greenpeace experience. You can watch.'

'You can't bring a barge alongside,' I said.

'We know. We've got two frogmen to plant the pyrotechnics: the security men won't be able to see what's on fire.'

'I'll obey orders, Vi. Honestly.'

'Then you and Sarkar can make up some drums and get us some smoke bombs. If you can manage radio fuses, you can fire them – you'll enjoy that.' Unshakeable, evidently. I left it to the WRAC and made a date with Sarkar to design and fabricate the gear. She'd even laid on scuba divers – clever Vi. There would probably be parachutists if required.

'On another matter,' said Sharkey, 'Cynthia has overcome her professional scruples, and we gave her a remote control camera. Should get us something for the file at both Party Conferences. Incredible how many of them are into S and M, Cynthia says.'

81

Serendipity – I physically bumped into Sarah, coming out of a West End Woolworth's which I do not ordinarily frequent, and made her drop her purse. When that was picked up, and she not seeming in any great hurry to go wherever she had been going, there was coffee, and then lunch, and in the upshot we spent the day together.

Some of the questions were a little difficult: she asked me if I saw much of Violet, and intended to see more of her. I felt she was trying in a way to preserve Violet's interests against the male. Obviously, though I responded perfectly truthfully, I was bound to sound evasive, because I could not confide in Sarah at this stage – if at all – what Violet and I were really up to.

'Violet and I,' I said, 'don't have anything going, Sarah. She went on her way.'

'But you keep on seeing her,' said Sarah.

'Look, we've both got involved in lobbying for refugee immigrants. That's what she went off to do.'

The unspoken conversation would have run, 'Father was smarter than I realised: if you weren't interested, you wouldn't go on about Violet'; 'Well, if I am it's mutual, but having been taken once I need to be careful with men, especially men of your family, simply out of self-protection.' Naturally we didn't say any of this, and she had a telepathic awareness that I knew her carnally, or almost, by looking at her fully and very nicely dressed; knowing that she knew made me a little sheepish too, because there was no way I could turn it off. But that wore off, and by the end of lunch we were being natural. She told me, rather defiantly, that she was illegitimate and brought up by her mother. She knew my family skeletons already, so I told her about the lectures, about Father Malachi, a bit about Sharkey, and about my nice Asian neighbours, and Oggie, and the riots, and we walked all the way back to my place – I showing her where the Roys' shop had been burned down. I realised that she was gentle as well as tough and pretty and that we often thought in tandem, as if we were dancing partners. We made supper jointly. When it got to the hour of decision I thought it tactful to offer to run her home.

'You don't have to,' said Sarah, leaving me to interpret: I

don't have to go at all, or, I can just as well take a taxi. Actually, I was supposed to be going to meet Sharkey and get on with some of the equipment, including the radio fuses and a broadband jammer, but if I said that, she'd return to the notion of an assignation with Violet, so I waited. I could always call Sharkey and put him off. But she put on her coat in a businesslike manner; I drove her home, there was quite a non-perfunctory kiss, and she said, 'Thank you, David' – thank you for not coming onto me tonight. I said I'd call her – I thought it had gone very well. I'd really made up my mind already about her, and I rather think that Sarah had made up her mind about me.

Violet, meanwhile, was totally in command. She did it very well. She had photographs of the prison ship – it was an old ferry, and there was a scale model in the Science Museum. She had made a personal reconnaissance, and she had blown up a map of the precise area down below the Essex marshes where they'd moored the thing. Apparently the hospitable Government reckoned that by putting it in a flat, swampy area with nothing much in sight, it would be easier to discourage breakouts. For our purposes this worked both ways.

'Now,' said Violet, 'there are three roads on the north-east bank. This one goes to the pier where they embark the prisoners. There are two launches tied up there. There's a fence round it, and gates on the road with a guard post and a telephone, but I don't see a radio antenna. This is the way the police will come if they're called.'

'And the Fire Brigade?'

'Probably, but there's a fire boat about two miles up river. Now, if you follow the road back, there's a right-angle bend over a drain. We can grease that bit of road thoroughly.'

'Charming,' I said. 'Go on, Vi.'

'This road goes to a little mud beach – not much cover, but there is a wartime pillbox, and quite a few people fish there. That's where we bring the van down with the canisters and the two divers. Now, the divers go in. First one of them goes over to the jetty and fouls the launch propellors with wire rope. He comes back, picks up No. 2 and the canisters and magnets and places them. Then he finds the underwater phone line to the ship – there is one, we've called it – and stands by to cut it.'

'Not a good idea, Vi. The dummy fire will be visible for miles. If you cut the phone, the crew will smell a rat and round up the immigrants. Leave it.'

'Good point. Boats – we've mustered three sizeable river yachts: one's a Thames barge. We're painting up a cabin cruiser to a reasonable resemblance of a police launch. We're also patching up an old rowing boat to use as a smoke layer. Now, having calculated wind and weather conditions, at zero minus twenty or so the rowing boat comes into position, towed by a yacht. Yacht anchors and pretends to lie up. The other two will be standing off, with the launch hidden between them. At zero minus five the divers come out and are recovered by the van, which stays in place, because it's carrying the radio control transmitter, *your* post. Communications – we use a CB band.'

'You don't – use two metres. CB is too damn close to the radio control frequency. It might set off the fuses.'

Violet made a note. 'We'll have to borrow what we can. At zero, you switch on your jammer and trigger the canisters. At the same time the yacht which towed in the rowboat lights fuses there and moves in, following the smoke. We give it five minutes. By then there should be near zero visibility. The three yachts feel their way in, in line ahead, with the launch, and the launch bullhorns the guard to evacuate the detainees.'

'If they don't?'

'The detainees are going to be briefed. One detachment rushes the guards – we're counting on the fire to thin them out down below, and they aren't armed. One detachment puts nylon fishing-line tripwires on the companion ladder. One detachment opens the cargo door. The divers will deliver a sledgehammer onto the end of a fishing line. They let them fish, I've checked. Then the yachts move down to the hard,

84

here, at the end of the third road, making smoke. The launch will follow pouring out petrol. It will fire the petrol when our squadron is clear. The detainees – they're all men – will have to wade ashore and board the furniture van.'

'Then what?'

'We're working on it.'

'It's a rather important part of the plan, don't you think?' said Sharkey, coming to life.

'I may be able to help here,' I said. 'First, Malachi's definitely on. He's got in touch with the parish priest, and they'll go on board together to set up the immigrant end.'

'Fabulous,' said Vi.

'Second, the parish priest can vanish them for you. He's got a pipeline into a community which holds retreats, about two miles away, but near the motorway. They've got cellars, a hall, bags of space, and they're a religious institution Immigration won't want to raid.'

Sharkey looked up rather wearily. 'How many people are in this thing already?' he said. 'I mean, yachtsmen, priests, two frogmen ex Greenpeace: it's a bloody army.'

'About twenty-five,' said Violet, looking a bit nervous.

'Forgotten my seminar?' said Sharkey. 'You have. Now David has been making up electronics – that's safe enough. You want Sarkar to buy smoke bombs, or steal them, plus filling drums with smoke mixture. Having a splendid time, aren't you? Ever occur to you that if twenty-five people are in on an operation, two hundred and fifty probably know about it? Do you seriously imagine the Grocer doesn't have snouts in the kind of liberal ecology circles you've been recruiting? Eh? Or that if your yachting friends are beetling around in a man-made fog with a hundred and fifty nervous immigrants, somebody isn't going to get killed?'

'We're going,' said Violet, setting her jaw.

'If you have to,' said Sharkey. 'Vi, it's a *good* plan, it shows a lot of feel for surprise, and you may have to do something like this eventually, so treat it as an exercise.'

And he suddenly became cloudcapped again, leaving the rest of us to stare at each other until the phone rang for Vi.

Frantic quacking at the other end – had she seen the late news?

Violet looked bitterly disappointed. Her jaw dropped – 'I see,' she said, and hung up. Sharkey nodded like a tin Chinaman.

'Well, Sharkey, that will please you,' she said. 'It's off. They've been given temporary admission after representations to the International Court of Justice – which is utterly unprecedented, so I don't believe it.'

'Doesn't it please you?' said Sharkey. 'I thought that was the object of the exercise.'

'You did this, didn't you, Shark?'

'The Minister got a letter – two, in fact. One from the Institute of Personal Information Studies and one from a Labour MP telling him he'd been in touch with the Institute. That one was a forgery – I happen to have some Commons paper. And Parliament reconvenes next week. International Court of Justice my Aunt Fanny. The Minister is one sodsucker we've got over a barrel. Now for the others. Lesson taken, Vi? I had to do something to head off paramilitary operations, but don't look so miffed. They'll come later, believe me.'

Sarkar looked a bit relieved, Violet bit her lip and looked really angry. I think she thought Sharkey didn't like a woman taking the initiative.

'If she wants to go for death or glory,' said Sharkey, as if she were a demonstration piece, 'she can always join the sodding IRA. They nearly did a job on the Grocer and half the palace eunuchs. They're also stupid pillocks and vicious with it. Like most terrorists. Now, shall we get on with the serious stuff?'

Sharkey agreed to add Fr Malachi to the team: 'But that's the last one,' he said, 'or we'll end up with a large leaky club.'

I suggested we might well need experts later on, for specific projects.

'Then we have an outer circle on a strictly need-to-know basis.'

Sharkey and Malachi got on splendidly. They saw things in

86

much the same way. We had to tell Malachi why Violet's little operation hadn't been needed. He understood better than I had done why Sharkey pre-empted it.

'They're young,' said Sharkey, as if he wasn't. 'They want to have a go at the Gadarenes, and they think of active resistance as a university rag. They've never had to deal with firearms, they don't realise Spivsville will fight, they're incautious and much too easily squashable. They have to learn.'

'They should talk to a Chilean girl I know,' said Malachi. 'All her brothers disappeared, she was raped repeatedly and tortured for six months, and she'd begun as a student, thinking it would be a great adventure. We aren't there yet in England, but that was simply Spivsville, as you call it, defending its positions. My grandfather thought war was going to be a great adventure when he enlisted in 1914. Do you reckon we can make them hard but not cruel?'

'Yes,' said Sharkey, 'but only if they don't lose the spark of wit when they realise what they're up against. Wit is an antidote to cruelty – the alternative is unfunny terrorism, isn't it?'

'I should know that,' said Malachi. 'I'm from Belfast.'

My problem was that Sarah was going to have to be let in, if things progressed, because of the Violet problem. The Shark looked grave.

'That's precisely how things leak, David. I see why the Roman Church insists on celibacy – celibates are harder to nobble.'

'That,' said Malachi, 'is a new interpretation of the Church's position.'

'She'd be useful, in view of her job,' I said, 'and I don't think she's been got at.'

'No,' said Sharkey, 'I agree. But I want to establish the principle. At this very moment little beady eyes are looking for the Institute of Personal Information Studies, which is why I didn't want to use it again. Never mind, in future it will be like the chap who crossed an elephant with a parrot – when it talks, they listen.'

'Burnside won't have gone to the police.'

'No, he'll have gone to the Grocer, and so to the Gestapo. But I don't think we gave them any leads. I hope they don't kill Mari Beauchamp.'

'You think they might?' said Malachi.

'Except for the fact that they know we're onto her, and they'd be giving us a Press coup. But Cynthia's warned her she's accident prone. It would be an accident, or a client,' said Sharkey. 'We felt it was only fair to warn her, and she's gone elsewhere. I feel guilty about using her name.'

9

I was woken by Sarah, bringing me tea: I was looking forward to waking first and finding her there, but this was as good or better. I pulled her in alongside and we drank the tea.

'There are,' I said, 'some things we need to settle. Like moving in for a while or getting married. I don't want to pressure you. Any preference?'

'I've got a strong preference for getting married. That is, if you want it. I've had enough of the other.'

'I do want it, so that settles that. I don't have any doubts, if you haven't.'

'I haven't,' said Sarah. I thought I knew her, but until I saw her asleep I hadn't realised how long her hair was, how like a Mughal painting she was. We had to get up and get on, however: Sarah was expected at work and I'd promised to go down and see Father. I asked Sarah if I should tell him.

'Yes, do. And tell me what his face is like when he hears,' she said.

'He's going to be as pleased as Punch. Does that bother you?'

'No. I've got no hard feelings in that quarter. I think I've come on a great deal since I was the little beddable secretary,' said Sarah. 'Get up now, David, and give me a lift — we can talk about the wedding tonight. It might be nice if a few people knew. I don't have relatives, but I imagine your parents will come.'

'Well, I'd like to ask Sharkey: and Mansur — I expect he'll insist on a Punjabi banquet. His wife loves cooking for people.'

Mother gave a little whoop: Father grabbed my hand and pumped it. 'Wisest thing you ever did, David. I know I was a bit clumsy about it, but it wasn't a bad idea.'

'No,' I said, 'it wasn't.'

Father waited until he got me on my own. Then he said: 'About the wedding, David. I know Sarah doesn't have any relatives, so presumably you'll be getting married from here.'

'We'll be getting married as quietly as possible, from my flat,' I said.

Father walked over to the window and turned his back to me, as he always did when it was going to be embarrassing. He said: 'David, I know you hate formal occasions. Just let me explain. I don't want to press you, but this wedding of yours could be extremely convenient if you're willing to play. Knowing how you tick, you probably won't be, but I'll tell you anyway. You know HMG bailed me out at the taxpayers' expense. They want desperately to re-establish my credibility – and London's, of course. Your getting married is an opportunity – that is, if you and Sarah could bear having a more formal occasion, you follow?'

'I follow,' I said. 'You want a really big tribal ceremony which will get media coverage – right?'

'Sounds terrible, I know,' said Father, 'but you get the idea, David.'

'Telegram from the PM, shaking hands for the camera with some of the palace eunuchs, Veuve Cliquot, caviare and Spivsville?' I said.

'Well, more or less. I'll pay for it – and the honeymoon. I hate to ask you. I imagine you want a Tibetan lama to officiate, or something. You don't owe me anything, so turn it down if you have to.'

Long shaggy ears. 'It depends,' I said, 'on Sarah. She might find a wedding financed by you a bit off colour, Father. But I'll ask her. And in any event I want Sharkey as best man – any PR objection?'

'None at all – excellent choice,' said Father. 'And, David, whatever you decide, I wish you both the best.'

I put it quite baldly to Sarah. She knew where I stood

90

vis-à-vis Spivsville. With Sharkey's consent I'd let her in over the activities of the Group. She simply opened her eyes wide and kissed me.

'You don't mind?' I said. 'You need to know what you're taking on.'

'I'm absolutely with you,' she said, 'and the only thing I don't want is you in prison. I couldn't be Winnie Mandela.'

When I told her about the paternal wedding plans, she wrinkled her nose and listened.

'Father,' I said, 'is about as sensitive as a Chieftain tank. I said I'd ask you, and now I'll call him and say thank you but no thank you.'

'Actually,' said Sarah, 'it would be odd rather than hurtful, and rather funny: do you realise, he'd have to give me away? Two years ago it would have been hurtful – now I'm going to say, ask Sharkey, before you turn it down – unless you really mind, David.'

'Why Sharkey?'

'Because I think he might find a way of using it,' said Sarah.

Sharkey listened very seriously while I told him the kind of junket Father was planning, a ghastly pig-rich grocerly Royal Ascot to put him back on the map. Then he said, 'We all have to make certain sacrifices. I shall understand if you don't feel able.'

'But you want me to do it.'

'I think so. I think we need you inside the occupying power. I think you should not only play the wedding for everything it will take, but ask to be received back into the fold like a good little quisling, kiss the Grocer's hand, bow down to the graven image which Nebuchadnezzar the King has set up, and become a really well-camouflaged mole, like me. We can't undermine these bastards from outside, and they're painfully trusting of Winchester and Cambridge.'

'Sarah?'

'He's got a point – provided David doesn't overegg the pudding by being fulsome. Dissimulation isn't his strong suit, Sharkey.'

'You,' I said, 'are already slated as best man.'

'Excellent,' said Sharkey. 'Now, I know you'll want to ask the Disciples – I wouldn't. We can celebrate afterwards. In the first place I don't want us linked as a group, in case one of us attracts attention from the occupying power.'

'You're thinking of Violet?' I said. 'It's all right – Sarah's briefed about her and me.'

'You said it, I didn't,' said Sharkey. 'As to Cynthia, it might be embarrassing if she met a client. You can ask Father Malachi – Dr Sarkar's going home to India for three months, so he won't be around. You can ask your Asian friends – that won't do any harm, provided they don't mind being patronised by a bunch of Tory racists.'

'I can ask Dr Wiston?'

'No objection to that. I think seeing the occupying power in full cry would crystallise the need to clobber them. At the moment he's hopping mad about what they're doing to his work and his patients, but he doesn't know how to hit back. Seeing them guzzling and giggling might be the catalyst. I see Wiston as an avenging angel one of these days.'

'He was at school with me, but I didn't know you knew him, Shark,' I said.

'I know him. He lanced a boil for me once, and in the middle of doing it, he blew up. He told me about your Mrs Roy and the burns, and about the shutting down of three wards at the hospital, and how he and his colleagues were pinning their hopes on the IRA to stop the attack on medicine.'

'Good old Wiston,' I said.

'So,' said Sharkey, 'we go ahead with the plan. Call your father and tell him that the potlach is on.'

Mansur gave me a British pat on the back which nearly knocked my wind out. 'Great!' he said. 'You now have regular relationship, which is how it should be. Also she is a great deal better than the last one: she looks like a Mughal lady.' I told him the resemblance had struck me, and invited him and his wife to the wedding.

He looked a little doubtful. 'It is a family occasion. We

should be out of place?'

'It's not a family occasion, and a few people out of place are exactly what is needed. You will see the Raj in all its scumbaggishness. Sharkey calls them the occupying power.'

'You know,' said Mansur, 'he is right. My father told me about these people. Now they have run out of colonials to bash, they bring back a little Empire here and bash their own people. You need a Gandhiji.'

'I'd trade him for Subhas Chandra Bose at the moment. Will you come, my friend, to give us a bit of support?'

'Yes, if you say so, David. It might annoy the sahibs. You know,' said Mansur, 'if you did it properly, Punjabi style, you would arrive with torches and musicians, riding on a horse. I think we will have a second wedding for you and make it really regular, if the girl agrees.'

'She'd be hurt if you don't,' I said, 'and she's very much on our side, Mansur. She could be our Rani of Jhansi.'

'Our ladies are tough,' said Mansur, 'Punjabi or Rajput, both, I am half Rajput, half Punjabi, and I appreciate fighting ladies.'

'Barring the Grocer?' I said.

'She is a yogini, not a woman,' said Mansur.

'I'd have said a rakshasa, but have it your own way. See you at the wedding. All her attendant ghosts and skeletons will be there.'

At every civilised wedding I have attended, the guests meet at the church and go from there to the food and drink. Father, given the object of the exercise, had other ideas – the guests would be received ahead of the ceremony (which gave ample time to meet evening television deadlines with the pictures) and would then be ferried to the church and back. The bride, of course, would make her entry at the church: according to Father's schedule, I would do the same. There would then be a reverse cortège, a second reception, and more picture opportunities. At what point the VIPs were to be injected into the process wasn't clear, but I had the impression they were being, as it were, spread throughout the proceedings. The Press, too, had been staggered to make sure they all came.

The impression was given that the bridegroom had spent the night under the parental roof. Actually I slept with Sarah at the flat, took her to the hairdresser to be picked up later by taxi and delivered to the back door along with the rented glasses, and collected Sharkey. We put the VW in the old stables and went inside to check that the medicine suits hired from the tribal tailor fitted us. Royal bloody Ascot was everywhere — the whole of the lawn was occupied by roustabouts putting up the big top. There were white tables and little knots of chairs, in case it did not rain. Crates started to go in full and come out empty while the red-and-white big top was still wobbling. Serfs carried in a red carpet, millipede-fashion, the giant maggot at the heart of Spivsville. Little yuppie ladies in jeans, based on the florist's van, By Royal Appointment, scuttled about bearing flowers. I wondered why I was putting Sarah through all this. At least the place had been so altered that she might not be bothered with memories — that last time she was here, it was as Father's mistress, not my bride, white dress and all.

Sharkey, well buttoned in and looking like a bookie's apprentice, helped me to suit up. It was the first time I'd seen him looking other than ruinous.

'Let them get inside,' said Sharkey, 'then we can nip down and stand on those crates. I think we should get a look at them before they see us.' Obviously he had the operation planned. Sarah, contrary to precedent and looking a little dishevelled in spite of the hairdresser, stuck her head in.

'Making sure you two are present and decent,' she said, and scuttled off.

'She looks nice,' said Sharkey, 'in a bra and slip.' He looked at his watch, produced a pocket chess set, and sat down at the table, leaving me to take the hint. At zero minus fifteen the big top was ready, the sceneshifters went and the waiters came, a quartet marched in with instrument cases, and finally Father, Moss Bross to the eyebrows and, I thought, viewing him from above, very slightly made up and tinted, made his way into the marquee, with Mother one pace behind wearing something simple and a bizarre hat: the King and Queen of

94

Trumps. And, on the dot, the first of a procession of hearses. Jesus, I thought, he's modelled this on a funeral. Sharkey put away the chess set. We watched the occupying power straggle in. Satie's *Gymnopedie* started up inside.

'Right,' said Sharkey.

The marquee had a kind of service entrance, where the crates were stacked. Sharkey carried them a few feet away and stacked them carefully against the canvas, in two stable piles. He mounted the first, produced a Stanley knife, and cut a peephole for himself. He then mounted the second and cut another for me. He took his place and motioned me to mine. 'Used to get a free view of the circus like that,' he whispered.

We were looking directly down the necks of the quartet. There was a red rope supported on brass stands, and beyond it was Father, the tides of Spivsville eddying around him, while Mother took cover behind him. There was the minicam, awaiting a signal, there were the photogs – one could spot the Press because they looked like ordinary human beings. Two chaps in dungarees were stationed with lights – one pup, one basher – and a pensive lady in jeans was presiding with a clipboard. I could spot the interviewer, because he was dressed halfway between the crew and the gentry, and taking the opportunity to stuff himself with nuts out of a bowl. They did it very nicely, lurking behind floral arrangements and seeing that the cables were clear of feet. The photogs were less tactful, and all of them were holding empty glasses. The sound background was peculiar – you could hear the quartet, but through it there was the unmistakable voice of the occupying forces, part Hooray Henry, and part a fragmented version of the Grocer, elocution lessons, chainsaw yowl and all – you expected them to yell *'koi hai?'* or call the waiters 'boy'. Mansur was right. Rhodesia and pre-Gandhi Poona had regrouped and were occupying England, and there was Father shaking them by the flabby, gloved or hairy, hand.

Then I saw Mansur himself, and his little wife. His turban had razor-edges, his beard was magnificent, his wife had a little round Sikh pillbox hat, and they'd come in traditional costume. Mansur's eyes were popping out of his head. They

95

gave namasti to Father. I heard a fishwifely female voice asking him if he was Indian, and had he been here long? He and his wife smiled courteously at the grocer clone and beat it behind a floral arrangement beside the bandstand. Mrs Mansur looked petrified. The move brought Mansur's turban within a foot of my eye.

'Psst!' I said. 'Courage, brother – help is at hand.'

Mansur looked round, spotted the hole and the eye in it and winked solemnly. Then he made a cutting-the-throat motion with his finger and led his wife in the direction of the refreshments. I heard him asking politely if they had soft drinks, and still more politely declining a cigarette from a Hooray Henry. Mansur was all right – he was playing the Martian anthropologist.

I knew most of this lot, or could place them – they were small fry, fragments of the Big Bang, the journeymen who manufactured all that negotiable paper. The next wave was chinnier and lower pitched – also less numerous, with fatter Mark I wives or daughter-sized Mark II wives: the Takeover Squad, before whom the journeymen fell back and quietened to a gibber, like Shiva's attendant ghosts. Father shook hands, slapped backs and was slapped, absorbed congratulations at his survival, and still the lights were not switched on and the minicam did not rise to an operating position. Next came two or three outsized Takeoverers, a little goblin with a white diabolico and a wizened little wife, and a large young man improperly dressed: the Big Money boys. The lesser Takeoverers deferred. Then there was silence in Heaven for the space of several seconds.

Somebody must have blown an inaudible trumpet. A pathway opened. Up it came a plump, thinlipped, varnished little man with a slightly hangdog expression. Behind came an angular, rather sad wife, a good deal taller than he was, and behind her two blue-suited goons with big feet; they looked like decent chaps who'd been long immunised. I could see caps and helmets at the tent entrance.

'That,' whispered Sharkey, 'is bloody Burnside, the Home Secretary – Cuntface to his friends. He's being moved to Trade and Industry. The Grocer thinks he's soft on niggers, and we know why.'

The lights went on, the minicam came up smartly, the interviewer put down his drink, Father bent in the middle, and the show was on the road.

'When I meet him,' I said, 'I'm going to ask him if that's Mari Beauchamp.'

'You do and you're a dead man,' said Sharkey. 'Anyhow, he won't stay for the wedding – only came for the photo opportunity. Well, Father's got what he wanted I reckon.'

'Wish we could get him photographed shaking hands with old Mansur Singh,' I said. 'The Grocer would give him a lecture in Cabinet.'

'Come on,' said Sharkey. 'Fags out – fasten seatbelts. We're on next. Is it true your Father has roped in a Bishop?'

'Shark,' I said, 'this tent is held up with guyropes, and you've got a Stanley knife …'

'No, David,' said Sharkey, 'later, later.'

There was in fact no bishop, though Father would undoubtedly have hired one if they were hireable. The Vicar was a spike and a Marian who reserved the Sacrament, used incense, and genuflected athletically, but at least he used Cranmer and not the Ladybird version of the marriage service. Before the rehearsal I had consulted Sarah – did she want a more feminist version?

'You mean "Our Mother who lives in Heaven?" No thank you, David.'

'I mean "obey" and all that.'

'I'm honestly not insecure enough to mind. A little while ago I might have. If we have Cranmer, let's have Cranmer.'

'Complete with the avoidance of fornication?'

'Yes – unless you think the Vicar would say disinfection instead of avoidance.'

I told her I doubted it, and we went on fornicating.

It was still beyond belief that she didn't resent all this – or wouldn't resent it when she actually had to go through it, having Father walk her up the aisle with the spivs mentally undressing her and the grocerettes assessing her points. It

97

was one thing to contemplate that, and another to do it in fact: I could fix my gaze on people I was glad to have there – the Mansur Singhs and Doc Wiston, who had quite possibly been on duty all night – but Sarah really had nobody. I was mortally scared she'd refuse when she saw the jump. I fidgetted and kept my eye on Sharkey, who was quite at his ease and seemed to have some source of information he hadn't communicated. Mother was there, beaming, dear waterproof lady – I wondered she did not knit while we waited. Wiston had a large unmedical young man with him whom I didn't know.

Finally Father, and Sarah, and two rent-a-kids from the neighbourhood in tow. The dress was really nice, her long hair hung down. It was a really witty dress – though it was white it was also thin, and shaped, and I thought there was even a hint of a pubic shadow – an allusion, a compliment or simply my imagination. Unfortunately she had the traditional dust sheet over her, hiding her expression, and I couldn't see if she were petrified or hopping mad. When Father cast off and she came alongside I could hear sniffings under the veil. It was only after a couple of seconds and a handsqueeze that I realised she was cracking with laughter and trying frantically to suppress it. I whispered, 'Steady, the Buffs.' The veil was going in and out convulsively.

'Ssh, we're on.' And we were. Nice service, no homily, prayer to Christ and His Blessed Mother to make it stick – 'O Love divine and golden', the register – Father sweating hard, Sarah looking volumes at him, then out in croc, to Widor's toccata. We dodged the ghouls and greeted the Mansur Singhs and Dr Wiston – the strange young man stayed aloof.

'Who's that, Joe?' I asked the Doctor.

'Tell you later. Best to you both,' – and he was jostled away by more horse faces. Mansur and Mrs Mansur lined up, hands joined, and Sarah scared him out of his wits by kissing them both. The Vicar wanted us off the premises sharpish (he had the size of Father's guests) so after a few flashbulbs we were shoved into one of the funereal cars. They'd brightened it up with white ribbon, but it still betrayed its dual purpose.

Back in the marquee the potlach continued: as it was Father's day, and none of the guests knew us, we were left pretty much alone with Sharkey – apart from photographs, cake cutting, and other fortunately nonverbal activities. The television crew ran a certain amount of tape, but once more they were clearly waiting.

'Watch it,' I said to Sarah, 'Father's got another VIP. Any moment now.'

'My God, I hope he hasn't talked the Witch of Endor into coming,' said Sarah.

'It might pay off if he has,' I said. 'Did you see that chap with Wiston? He looks like a would-be assassin. That *would* put Father on the map.'

Never make jokes. At that moment the noiseless trumpet blew, the occupying power fell back like the waves of the Red Sea, and in came another of them, slightly different in shape from the first, sprayed with the same varnish but this time wifeless. Behind him came another pair of goons, but he motioned them away (they were spoiling his entrance, I suppose). He marched up to Father and, to the full media coverage, pumped his hand.

'Nutkin, Minister of Health,' whispered Sharkey. The chap turned to us. 'Meet my son and daughter-in-law, Minister,' said Father. 'Gladameecha,' said the Minister. It was like shaking pectoral fins with a codfish. A media voice said, 'Kiss the bride, Minister.' I was about to whisper to Father that if he did, he'd attend the next Cabinet in a wheelchair, when Sarah tripped forward, obviously about to clasp him to her bosom and give him an embarrassing smacker.

But she never connected. Between her and the Minister there loomed up the form of Wiston's stranger. With the cameras rolling, he said, in a level but very audible voice, 'You bloody little pillock. My father waited two years to get into hospital because of your NHS cuts and he didn't make it. I hope you rot in Hell.'

The Minister swallowed, then ducked – the audience gasped, the media cheered inaudibly, the two goons, who'd backed off as instructed, made a dive – but the gatecrasher

99

was too quick for them. He was out under the wall of the marquee.

'Well,' said the Minister, 'I'm sorry about that.'

'I'm not,' said Sarah brightly, 'I expect it happens all the time, doesn't it?'

Father went up to the TV crew. I could hear him trying to get them to exercise some civic responsibility, and the lady producer gentling him. Nutkin gave a sickly grin and plunged into the crowd who were waiting to condole and stay him with flagons. I looked for Wiston, but he'd apparently gone: he'd no business to do that. It was only when we drifted out that I saw two groups had formed – one round the Minister, now under close escort, and the other round Dr Wiston, who was giving a Press conference.

When he'd finished giving them the whole case history, Sarah and I tackled him. We spoke simultaneously. I said, 'That was a rotten trick.' Sarah said, 'Nice work, Doctor.'

'I'm sorry,' said Wiston. 'I didn't like spoiling your wedding. But I thought it was the one occasion he had a chance of getting to the swine with the Press there. It'll make all the papers, the TV, and the wire services. I'm too angry over casualties to follow Queensberry Rules.'

'Quite nice,' said Sharkey, grinning like a wooden Indian.

'Did you know about that, Shark?' I asked.

'He cleared it with me,' said Sharkey. 'I thought it was quite a good idea. Pinpricks help, you know.'

10

So we drove in style to the airport, handed in the vouchers for an expensive honeymoon in Mykonos to be refunded, and went back to the flat. Sharkey had brought the Volkswagen back, and with it the Mansur Singhs, who invited us all to dinner, and the jamboree was over. I gave Fr Malachi a running commentary on it. His comment struck me as perceptive: 'You have to find these people ridiculous, don't you, so as to keep your hands off them? It's not a bad way of dealing with contempt and loathing. The hard part for me is that they're human, the Occupying Forces, and we're supposed to accord them the privileges of human beings.'

'That would have been true of the Nazis, or Caligula,' I said, 'and it makes me wonder if I can keep up the bodhisattva route. The ninja route would be easier.'

Malachi felt that it wasn't ignoble to want to murder these people, because I wasn't mad about things they'd done to me, but about things they had done to England, to Mrs Roy, to the people on waiting lists and in scummy bedsits and dole queues. Sharkey listened and took a more pragmatic view – he sympathised, about avenging being more moral than revenge, but if I'd bide my time and concentrate on practicalities, I could help him combine benevolence with come-uppance. 'They're living on candy-floss,' he said, 'and candy-floss melts when it rains. All it needs is a little help from us.'

There was one other thing – a large brown envelope from Father. If we'd gone on the junket he booked for us we'd have found it when we got back. As it was, Sarah and I opened it in bed, over breakfast. I passed the paternal letter over to her.

My dear David,

I know you are going to maintain your married responsibilities on an academic salary, and that you don't wish to join the business. On the other hand, sexual intercourse is apt to produce children, and whether you like it or not you will eventually be my heir. Rather than waiting until I die, and donating a large part of it to the Government, my solicitors have found a device to transfer a considerable holding to you which, in their opinion, does not attract capital transfer tax. Moreover the manner of transfer ensures that you cannot in a fit of philosophy make it over to the Dalai Lama or the Irish Republican Army, which would be your equivalent of wasting it in riotous living. The value of the capital sum will vary with the market – the estimated annual income will be about £250,000 before Tax. I can't impose conditions on the use you make of this, but you might at least consider that I earned it – you didn't. Apart from fiscal considerations (it will save me Tax) you can take it as a gesture of appreciation for having taken the wedding in good part. I'd also describe it as a gesture of my genuine affection and respect, but you would probably consider that over the top.

Your loving Father.

Sarah read the letter. I said 'He's bought me a commission in the army of occupation, and he's apparently fixed it so that I can't even give it away. With that sort of money one could fix an election, or hire hit-men to waste the entire cabinet.'

Sarah said, 'He may also mean what he says about affection. It's the only way he knows of showing it. I don't think he imagines he's made a yuppie of you, and you can spend the £250,000 on subversion if you like. Otherwise it's just Monopoly-money.'

Sharkey, unexpectedly, was delighted, and said that the Lord was delivering them into our hand.

'You want me to take it?' I said.

'Apart from the fact that you can't refuse it, yes. It makes you a credible investor. What I have in mind is going to need someone with a credit rating. So you sell that rusty car and buy a Ferrari, you shake all the clammy little hands that people extend to you – even the Grocer will treat you as kosher if you look like a donor to Party funds – and you talk about Free Enterprise in a rather nasty counter-tenor. You're our mole, David.'

Sharkey's idea seemed to be that I was to stage an indefinite prolongation of that ghastly wedding, and I told him so.

'All right, all right,' he said, 'you're a rotten actor, stay as you are. But you can't keep 250 big G's under the bloody bed, so establish your credit as an investor. That's really the only part I'm going to need when we move.'

And so I returned to the class, and came alive: Sarah attended it, at her own request, and was embraced by Cynthia. She also joined the Disciples and was embraced by Violet, so that was all right. Cynthia had come back from the Party conferences with some deadly snapshots and two videotapes. Sarah, dear girl, put Cynthia's activities down to revolutionary self-sacrifice and said she admired anyone who could have sex with those creeps in the public interest.

'It's all right,' said Cynthia, 'I don't usually need to have sex with them – they're mostly far too kinky to appreciate that.'

As for Sharkey, he kept reiterating that candy-floss melts when it rains, and reminding us of what happened to the Martian invaders in *The War of the Worlds*.

'Look, Shark,' I said finally, 'don't interpret this as distrust on my part, but don't you think you could let us in on the grand strategy? I mean, if you're brewing a nation-changing conspiracy all on your own, you might as well not have us around.'

'Patience,' said Sharkey, 'you all have parts to play – but I don't want to particularise prematurely.'

'Which means,' said Violet, 'that he's been doing some fishing, but apart from being able to blackmail a few VIP's, he hasn't got a good line.'

'The line is simple,' said Sharkey. 'It's the detail which takes time.'

'If it's simple, give us a seminar,' said Violet.

Sharkey thought about that one. Then, laboriously, he erected a blackboard.

'Anybody read *The Count of Monte Cristo* lately?' he said. 'If not, it's the course textbook. Dantes escapes from prison, finds a treasure, and arranges for all his old enemies to scupper themselves through their own weaknesses. That's our model – moral and economic jiu-jitsu.

'Now, the line. Proposition One – the scumbag society runs on candy-floss. It doesn't create sources of wealth, it pushes paper around. It runs on deficits and credit. Ergo, it's inherently unstable and is headed for a God-awful crash. So as to limit the mischief it can do before that happens, we need to add a push. Objection: that's going to cause total confusion and make things a lot worse for ordinary people. Reply: as it's going to happen anyway, it's best to get it over in a controlled manner – so that the scumbags can't wriggle out by setting up Fascism or starting a third World War. We simply move the inevitable forward.

'Proposition Two: *what* the scumbags push around isn't wealth but information – paper, and now, coded data in data banks. And information is vulnerable – you can misdirect it, introduce errors into it, delete it: right? Right. Now there is as a result an immense amount of information-based fraud, ranging from insider trading to misdirecting remittances – low-grade computer fraud. Some of the higher-level methods are the main occupation of the post Big Bang elite; the lower level methods are simple stealing, from insider employee fraud to computer hacking and fiddling automatic tellers: most of business simply writes this off for fear of upsetting confidence, as it does shoplifting.

'Proposition Three: both classy fraud and vulgar fraud, and the measures taken to prevent them, are concerned with tampering with information so as to shift the Monopoly-money out of its present situation into the fraudster's account. In other words, fraud is diverting information for someone's benefit. Question: what would happen if information were to be diverted at random, not for anyone's benefit, so that paper assets were transferred into the stratosphere, or into a Black

104

Hole? Operation Monte Cristo consists in designing the Black Hole and causing large sections of the candy-floss to dissolve and fall into it. I hope that's intelligible to everyone. It needs, obviously, at least as much ingenuity and chutzpah as your average big time City swindle, and then some – which is why I'm proceeding slowly. After all, if fraud is the second oldest discipline, financial sabotage is a relatively new one. Its peculiarity, and its strength, is that it isn't designed to make a profit – it's designed to make phoney wealth disappear. Any questions?'

I don't know if everyone got the idea: I did, and it struck me as masterly – and feasible.

'If you're going to fiddle the City's computers and make the Walls of Jericho tumble, just like that,' said Cynthia, 'why do you need blackmail information?'

'Because,' said Sharkey, 'we're going to need a few controlled individuals, plus the ability to create diversions. Violet's little scheme to spring her immigrants depended on a series of diversions: you nearly always need them. Now, are you ready to give me time, or do you want me to rush in and start something at half-cock? Good. We now have David as a wealthy investor. That's a start.'

'David,' said Sarah, 'isn't going to get sent down for fifteen years, and we aren't going to have to move to the Costa del Sol, so that you can get even with the Grocer.'

'No dishonesty on David's part will be required,' said Sharkey, 'and since nobody will benefit from any operations we conduct, nobody is going to be prosecuted – except possibly myself, if they put a trace on the operations I conduct. Now, can we leave it, think about it, and construct scenarios? I'm open to all reasonable suggestions.'

Well, I thought, a voice will be heard in Ramah, yuppies weeping for their bundles of Monopoly-money, because they are not. And when that happens, they'll do the Grocer and all others in like case offending. I want to be there, I want to be there.

Pinpricks were going to be the order of the day. Dr Wiston

105

came round for coffee, looking thoroughly miserable. He found us sitting in armchairs, with Sharkey playing the concertina and giving a seminar on it.

'It was invented,' said Sharkey, 'by Wheatstone, who also invented the Wheatstone bridge.'

Wiston looked as if he couldn't care less.

'Not content with having the NHS wrecked, and us having to turn people away, they're sending a VIP round to patronise the sick and show their concern. Next Thursday,' he said.

Sharkey showed immediate interest.

'What VIP? Nutkin?'

'Won't tell us on security grounds.'

'It couldn't be Her Nibs in person?' said Sharkey.

'Probably a minor royal,' said Wiston. 'The Grocer only ventures out in a tank – too scared of the populace.'

'Well, have they locked a toilet and changed the seat for one whereon no man ever sat? No? Then it isn't a royal. It could be the Grocer – showing caring and all that. Do you want to borrow a rifle?'

'I can't,' said Wiston. 'The constraints of medicine. Wish I could.'

'Blowpipe? Crossbow? Wrong time of year for a deathcap mushroom, I'm afraid.' Wiston shook his head. 'Tip off the IRA?'

'And get my patients killed?' said Wiston.

'Tell me,' said Sharkey, 'what you're putting on.'

'Walkabout – patronising a few disabled kids. The Administrator thought it would be nice if some of then sang.'

'Sang what?'

'Nymphs and Shepherds – or a hymn, I suppose,' said Wiston.

'What hymn?'

'The kids like "What a Friend we have in Jesus",' said Wiston. 'Perfect,' said Sharkey. 'Tell me, are the kids reliable?'

'Well, they're bright – and mischievous,' said Wiston.

'In which case,' said the Shark, 'they need an accordionist to lead the singing. And a few rehearsals. I volunteer.'

106

'Don't forget,' said Wiston, 'that this is a hospital. These kids are patients. That comes first.'

'Of course,' said Sharkey, 'but you do see the window of opportunity? Just a gentle prod, to make the Grocer's day? No rough stuff – just some singing: if it's a harmless royal, we give them Jesus. If it's the Grocer, we give her a short, sharp shock. *You*'d better know nothing about it, doc. When can I rehearse the choir? Quid pro quo for your wedding caper?'

Sarah and Wiston were both apprehensive: I arranged to borrow a white coat and a badge and watch with the nursing staff. It was as well that I got there early, because on the day the whole place was crawling with spooks. The kids in bed were all potted, sprayed and beribboned, the flowers had been sent in, the Administrator was neatly polished like one of Lewis Carroll's oysters, and Sharkey had had three sessions with the Gospel Choir, who were lined up now in a sort of gallery, normally used for storing bedsteads. There was a curtain to one side, and behind that, I divined, was Sharkey.

Where I was, in the sideward, I was surrounded by exhaustion and indignation. These people had had almost 24 hours on duty, patients in other wards still open were bursting their bladders, an operating list had been cancelled, simply to make a Roman holiday. The minicams were waiting downstairs. It had to be the Grocer. No royal would have been so inconsiderate. I wondered how many of the staff were in on the plan. The limousines arrived, the Administrator went to genuflect. One of the nurses looked out of the window (I couldn't see from where I was) and gave the high sign toward the curtain. Some of them evidently knew.

Then we heard that unspeakable voice, three minicam operators came in backwards, and the Grocer was upon us, collecting royal bows and curtseys. A nurse muttered, 'Thinks she's the bloody Queen.' Sheepish children were patronised on-camera: 'Isn't that a splendid bear – did your mother give you that?' – the lot: adjurations to get well quickly, then, to the cameras, 'Have we got all we want? Splendid.' Administrator steering the Grocer to a chair. 'They're going to sing? Splendid!' The invisible concertina squealed 'What a

107

Friend we have in Jesus', the children rose, and they sang. Clearly, sweetly, making every word count, ten angelic little Jamaicans singing their hearts out – and holding typewritten words in front of them.

And these were the words they sang.

Get back on your broomstick, Grocer –
    don't you think it's time you went?
Go and snuggle up to Botha,
    go and grope the President!
You've done nicely for your flunkeys,
    buggered up the NHS,
shown you do not give a monkey's
    for us poor folks in distress.

I thought the double-take was extraordinarily slow – it may have been the Jamaican accent, or the Grocer was intent on looking caring for the cameras. Then there were chuckles among the staff and the Press, mouths dropped open – and the Caligulous smirk on the Grocer's face turned to a lizard-like glare. Snakes appeared in the coiffure. She was about to start for the door. But the angelic choir hadn't finished yet.

All those spivs and snobs and wankers,
    all the yuppie middle class,
all those inside-dealing bankers
    hunker down to kiss your ass.
When the IRA gets lucky
    we will scrape you off the floor –
shut the lid and pull the handle
    hear that canting voice no more …

Out stumped the Grocer, the goon squad rushed for the gallery, finding the door locked and falling over surplus bedsteads, and from the entire staff there rose a storm of laughter and clapping. By the time they got the door open, there were only demure choristers in the gallery.

'Hope I haven't cost you your job,' said Sharkey, lying back in the chair next day.

'I doubt it,' said Wiston, 'the Administrator's hopping mad, but staff morale went up ten whole points. Have you seen the

Press?' He held up the *Mirror*: HOSPITAL GREETS PM WITH INSULT SONG. The *Sun* had BLACK CHOIR SPITS ON PM. The *Guardian* had a quite jolly account of an 'extremely insulting and personal ditty … the Prime Minister had obvious difficulty in controlling her anger, and left immediately'. Nothing in *The Times*.

'Any assignment of responsibility?' said Sharkey.

'We told the police that the choirmaster was a volunteer from the Council social centre – obviously a Trot.'

Copies of the tape were circulating in Fleet Street, and quite a few pubs appeared to have started singing hymns.

'Awful, vulgar doggerel,' said the Shark, 'but appropriate, I think. Did you see Medusa's face?' He played a little roulade on the concertina. 'There have been occasions in history when a song has tipped the balance – not this one, I'm afraid, but "Ça Ira", "Lilliburlero": always have a laugh over that one – the dictionary says the words are gibberish: actually they're Irish – "up with the lily, we won the day". Have you noticed, when the English sing protest songs there's always an Irishman behind it?' And Sharkey squeezed the concertina and began to sing 'The Sean Bhean Bhocht'.

As for the Grocer, sources tell me she was all for issuing a D notice, abolishing the local Council and cutting the hospital's budget. With a by-election coming, wiser counsels prevailed, but members of the Opposition took to whistling 'What a Friend we have in Jesus' on suitable occasions. The tune was even heard occasionally in Cabinet when things got more than usually Caligulous.

11

Through all this, with only one gap for the actual wedding, the classes droned on. The physicists were doing splendidly, and when we got to Kant and the non-Kantian models – Bergson, Leibnitz and so on – I let them take over the running. Malachi was as earnest as ever – could he actually *see* the extradimensional universe where 'All is always Now'? I told him yes, probably, if he undertook the appropriate exercises, though I couldn't guarantee it. That led to a class debate on how far unusual states of mind could be regarded as a source of knowledge. Could philosophers use LSD as marine biologists use skindiving? I told them to stay off psychedelics and stick to yogas – Christian yogas, if they wanted to take the trouble to study the Hesychasts, Buddhist yogas if they wanted to talk to a living tradition. The physicists told Malachi he didn't need to *see* it – after all, he was a priest, and he didn't expect to see God – because they could show it to him by mathematics. No participation from Matthew. He seemed far more interested in Cynthia, and that bothered me.

In fact, I spoke to her. 'He's a priest, and a pretty muddled one with all the non-Thomist stuff he's hearing. I can't help it if he kicks over his vows eventually, but I'd rather it was after he left my class – otherwise he'll be the last ordinand we get.'

'If his vows were silly in the first place,' said Cynthia, 'he might as well find out now. I've not been chasing him, David, but helping muddled people deal with sexuality is my *job*. I don't want to say no if he asks me – I promise not to charge him.'

111

'Later,' I said, 'not while you're both in the bloody class.'

'Later he'll go back to the menagerie and run out of courage,' said Cynthia. 'He'll never make a hard-wired, fully paid up, Y-fronted celibate. I'm actually quite good at reading people: Malachi, yes – Matthew, no.'

'Cynthia, I asked you to lay off it.'

'And his Tarot's got the Fool, the Lovers, and the eight of swords reversed.'

'Are you going to do as I ask, or do I have to boot you both out of the class?'

'I could ask him to hear a confession.'

'Don't do anything so bloody mischievous. You'll drive him round the bend.'

'All right, I was kidding. And there's only three weeks of this term left. You've got Sarah, Vi's got a Cause, Malachi's got a Vocation. Matthew's got nothing but doubts and hormones.'

'Well, if you're right,' I said, 'don't let him get stuck as a masochist or something.'

'I won't: I only play it that way if they enjoy it, or use it as magic to get out of the body image – I'm quite skilled at getting rid of guilt feelings. That's why I don't like working with politicians – they don't have any, which makes them nasty, not playful,' said Cynthia. I told her she should write a textbook: she knew more psychotherapy than the non-playing coaches.

Garner rabbiting away about setting a more searching examination: why set something like 'What do you understand by "real" in the context of science and in the context of ordinary experience?' Wouldn't it be more extending to ask 'Compare and contrast Wittgenstein's and Berkeley's concepts of the real?'

No, it bloody wouldn't, because I wanted thinking, not regurgitated textbook. And this question, 'Can a politician operate as a philosopher?' Wasn't that political science, which isn't in the syllabus? So it went on, rabbit, rabbit, rabbit until I finally said 'Look, Sir, would you mind awfully sodding off and letting me get on with this paper? I want to know what they've learned and whether they've acquired some thoughts as well as information – right?'

Yes, of course, he saw – difficult to examine for wisdom, but I was entitled to try – original idea, the mark of a natural if unorthodox teacher – exit, pursued by a tripehound. I hoped Cynthia wouldn't get him, and me, fired through Inferior Benevolence. PRIEST LOSES VIRGINITY AT 'PHILOSOPHY' CLASS – I could see it in the *Daily Fart*.

Then he popped his head in again to congratulate me on my marriage and invite us both to dinner. Someone had given him an extra big carrot and he wanted to share it. I wrote down the address of his burrow.

Instead, Sarah and I had Sharkey round to dinner. We got, inevitably, a seminar – one I wanted to hear, because I didn't share Sharkey's overconfidence that he could inflict more than a few scratches on the system. Sharkey thought otherwise.

'First of all,' he said, 'there's a whacking amount of computer fraud actually going on. One British bank lost around £6 million, but it's trying to keep the thing quiet. An American securities company lost $10 million – ditto. These weren't done by hackers – the hackers we know about are mostly doing it for fun: planting Trojan Horse programs on NASA, reading Prince Philip's mail. They're extremely clever, extremely good programmers, and they're having a ball. From which we've got to assume there are hackers we don't know about, like Intelligence services – they hack for information. I'll bet my wig the Russians are super-hackers: it goes with chess. So it is possible in principle and in fact to get into most systems, protected or not, and encrypted or not. But the fastest way in is from the inside. The actual frauds are nearly all employee jobs. Either they see the big chance, or they stroll into the computer room and somebody's left the access codes lying around – or the firm's still using the original passwords which came with the machine, and those are in the instruction manual. Nine times out of ten, if you try them, they still work.

'Now the frauds I've heard about so far are all quite

pathetically simple – transferring cash to dummy suppliers and things like that. I don't know of any case where someone has tapped into the codeword lexicon stored in the machine, but there's one there, and it has to be tappable. So although there are 3×10^8 combinations for any 6-digit code word, in actual fact they tend to use guessable combinations, which one can program the search to try first – it's a little like the *Times* crossword – or they simply don't take enough care. If you can't get in that way, there may be servicing entrances, or you may be able to get hold of one code word and find that there's no barrier against using a Trojan Horse – especially if you can tap into a legitimate user. So feasibility is quite high, even without any elaborate hacking methods.

'As to scratching the surface, the automated clearing system between British banks moves about £30 billion a day. If you could link this into the international financial message service, how long do you reckon it would take to empty Britain of Sterling? It's been computed at fifteen minutes. Now a fraudster would be shifting it into his own dummy accounts, he'd have to draw it out, and it would eventually be traceable. What if it didn't go to Sharkey, Inc., but into a Black Hole? Utter chaos.

'Now I'm responsible for stopping people from pulling computer frauds on your Father. He sends me to all the top secret briefings on countermeasures – very handy. One thing I've done has been to get the security boys to conduct a survey of how exactly people store their records – are they on tape, in a memory, or duplicated on microfilm? Mostly they're duplicated on tape. So to read them you have to feed them into the machine. Suppose the machine has been parasitised to alter the tapes it reads? That can be done – result, chaos.

'Finally, there are crabs and viruses. Crabs are a bit of a joke – they appear in one corner of the screen and eat the display bit by bit: very bad for morale if your client's watching the performance. Viruses get in via the housekeeping instructions and gradually rot away either the data or the programming – and they're contagious: they can be fixed so that they are passed on to any other system which accesses

114

the infected system. Crabs give themselves away and make it obvious someone's been playing silly buggers with the system. Viruses don't until it's too late. Conclusion – gold wasn't perishable, paper was easily duplicated and forgery was difficult – very few Banks could be wiped out by a fire unless they were damn careless. But the informational candy-floss on which the entire Scumbag Society's been erected is vulnerable, alterable, buggerable and, in fact, a sitting pigeon. Among all that amateur hacking talent, not one youngster has appreciated the revolutionary potential of his skills. Most of them want to be yuppies too. That, lady and gentleman, is my starting-point.'

Sarah gave him a long clap. I told her I'd been mistaken – I thought she was a little sorry for all those hot-handed Tory voters who worshipped the Grocer into office. 'All I want to see,' said Sarah, 'is the entire litter jumping out of the windows of 10 Downing Street and running for their lives, with the enraged bourgeoisie after their blood. They've earned it, David. They'll want a Health Service to deal with the cuts and bruises, they'll wish their kids could still buy their way into College. It will be a great big Biblical come-uppance – like the last Judgment.' I told her we'd try to arrange it for her.

As the end of the course approached, we Garnerised ourselves by going back over the syllabus and filling in gaps. That left us with dialectical materialism: I did the history, the class decided that the dialectical part was alive and well, though you could hear Hegel, Marx and Engels turning in their graves when they dragged in Prigognine and the superpositional resolution of opposites. It was the materialism on which the axe fell. Also for a year or so now I hadn't once had the obligatory young political Marxist, and had to fill in for him or her myself. All we got out of that was a heated discussion on extrapolations from philosophy to society. Garner had to put his head round the door at the precise moment that I was impersonating a hardline Marxist-Leninist for instructional purposes, and the expression on his face and the additional

115

protrusion of his eyes showed that he'd totally misunderstood the exercise.

'Er – hah – *you* aren't a Marxist, are you, David?'

'No, and I'm not Socrates: if you'd put your head in at the start of the course you'd have heard my impersonation of Socrates. I do it in a bath towel. I meant to bring a beard for Marx, but it got ruined in the laundromat.'

'Er – hah – most amusing. I admire your original way of putting it over: method acting in academia, hah?'

Εἴθε γένοιμην – would I had a house in bloody Milton Keynes and a nice job at the Open University: with no white rabbit sodding around, snooping on my classes, and generally doing his Alice in Wonderland act. Sarah seemed to like the idea, and suggested I try to realise it.

The paper got by in the end. Garner held it at arm's length and read it out like a proclamation.

'Write brief essays on THREE of the following:

1. Monads
2. Anselm, ontological argument, and hyperreal numbers
3. 'History is bunk' (Henry Ford)
4. The meaning of 'meaning'
5. Causality and Kant's a-prioris
6. The philosophical implications of computer science
7. 'This statement is a lie'
8. Just wars

'Are you quite sure you aren't bowling to particular students, David? I mean, you've got two maths graduates who know what hyperreal numbers are: I don't suppose the others would know one from an astrolabe. And 'just wars' is playing to the two RC priests – *and* moral philosophy wasn't really in the syllabus.'

'Could you do the paper?' I said, sweetly.

'Er – huh – probably not – not my subject.'

'Well, if you'd attended the class and heard the range of the discussions, and if you were of reasonable intelligence and

116

listened, you would be able to pass. And you'd have difficulty in picking which of the choices gave you most scope. The maths people have learned the relevance of classical philosophy to their subject, the priests have learned that maths are a philosophical subject, and the arts people have had a crash education in mathematical physics. That's called broadening the mind.'

'Not sure I see this course as a mental shoe-stretcher,' said Garner, 'they are supposed to be learning philosophy.'

'Instead of which,' I said, 'they've been bloody doing it, for themselves.'

'Er – huh – we don't have an external examiner, David. I have to trust you to plough them if your pedagogic exercise fails to impart knowledge – not that I think it will fail, you know, greatest respect for creative teaching but er – huh.'

'I'll plough them,' I said, 'if they copy out the textbook. I'll pass them if they show evidence, however slight, of using what they've heard. Right?'

'Have to give some credit for knowledge,' said Garner.

May beets grow in his belly, God forbid.

'Eh?' said Garner, popping his head in again.

'I said, it beats the stuff they see on the telly.'

'Quite, quite. Sure they'll do you credit, er – huh.'

Write a brief essay on the reasons why the Devil will choke all academic Deans and show your results to the examiner.

I haven't said much about Sarah as a wife. When she was servicing Father she struck me as a rather wound-up, tragic person and probably abominably accident prone – Jane Eyre in jeans. But either she had changed with a rush, or I had got it horribly wrong because of the setting. She was very affectionate, which I'd guessed, self-contained, and gentle and compliant without being pliable, sexually creative and adventurous without any reservations except that it had to be with me, and intelligent in a way that took her straight to the centre of anything she talked about. She was also tough, and we were inordinately happy. Altogether a colossal bonus, and here was I refusing to look twice at her because I thought she was another of Father's takeover bids. Well, at that time I'd been right – Father didn't appreciate what he had, and wouldn't have liked her if he'd realised. His demands on women struck me as roughly similar to his demands on staff – cheerful, non-demanding yes-persons to whom he need not have obligations. He'd have run a mile from any mistress with some self-esteem, and he made sure that when he was around Sarah didn't acquire any. Fortunately she beat him to it. I think the self-esteem came first and the summary sacking as his girl-friend followed. 'Girl-friend' sums it up – a woman would have been too threatening: after all, Father and Antrobus and hoc genus omne saw themselves as 'the boys' and called one another 'old boy'. So by analogy women remained 'girls' up to pensionable age. Father was a boy, all right, but Sarah, luckily for me, was a woman. Father probably called her 'baby' – he needed a brisk encounter with Germaine Greer. Sarah didn't need one – she took womanhood naturally now, so no need to be strident about it, and we were pretty happy with one another as Adam and Eve persons.

What was more, she suddenly blossomed out, as if she'd got rid of John Bunyan's burden. One day, when I told her she was good, and a natural, and just the woman I wanted, she said, 'Yes, I know I'm good like that, but so are a lot of women. What you really want is something else – isn't it called a dakini?'

'Yes, or a śakti.'

'Meaning a woman who can actually make you see?'

'Yes. Have you been talking to Cynthia?'

She nodded, as far as one can when horizontal.

'Have you ever had Cynthia?' she asked.

'You mean, before we got together?'

'Before or after, it doesn't matter: I'm not being jealous. I just want to know if she can do as she says.'

'You're still jealous of Violet.'

'Well, she's competition: Cynthia isn't. I gather you have had her, then.'

'A couple of times,' I said. Well, I know she was my student

118

and in a fiduciary relationship, but she was also a grown woman and a virtuoso.

'And can she do what she says she can? I mean, not just big orgasms and nice kinky games?'

'She can indeed. But so could you.'

'Then why don't I?' said Sarah. 'I'm just as orgasmic and probably just as kinky.'

I explained that the dakini thing, which I hadn't really understood until I'd experienced it, was something quite different from Adam and Eve sex.

'More ritualistic?' said Sarah.

'Ritual in sex usually means playing charades. I'd say more devotional.'

'And I could learn, and we could play it that way sometimes?'

I told her yes, she could, and I'd like that more than anything.

'Then we can either send me to Cynthia and let her teach me, or ask her to join us sometimes, or both,' said Sarah. 'And let me ask her, so she'll know she isn't cutting in on me.'

We did both, the second on quite a number of occasions. If that turns you off, it's because you have no idea what the exercise is about. It was always going to be there for us whenever the straight Adam and Eve ran out. Although non-attachment is part of it, so the Masters claim, we found that You and I fuels He and She and the step beyond that, and Cynthia could bow out and leave us and return to the temple where she danced, while we went on our journey of exploration.

12

Sharkey's next move was to start a financial tipster sheet. He secured Father's approval – we welcome enterprise in our staff, provided it doesn't involve the Firm or interfere with their duties: Sharkey told him it was a spare-time effort and gave the Firm a free subscription. His name didn't appear on the masthead. The editors were an analyst at the Bank of Hokkaido, Mr Matsushiro, and an eminent Swiss broker, Mr Max Erlenmeyer. There was also a Mr Dwight R. Hunnycut.

I asked him who the hell they were, and why he was doing it. 'Well,' said Sharkey, 'Matsushiro's wholly imaginary, Erlenmeyer agreed under persuasion, and Dwight was my room-mate at Stanford – if he finds out, he's too good a sport to complain. *All* these tipster sheets have fake backers: some of the big names in America are consortia of journalists. As to why, time will tell. First we acquire credibility.'

He started by sending the thing around gratis to the financial press and some City houses, with subscription slip enclosed.

The first issue opened with some sober comment on commodities, a strategy on spreads, a company evaluation – all routine stuff. It ended with a paragraph on impending takeovers, predicting two big ones. 'Our takeover predictions,' it said, 'are based on the analysis of stock buying patterns, not on rumour or inside information. Investors will appreciate that if the appearance of our predictions causes large price movements, bid timing and bid completion may be affected.'

They were – in fact, there was a minor uproar. An American buyout of half Britain's truck industry, on which the Grocer was especially keen, blew up all over the Press (without acknowledgement to the tipsheet) and spilled into Parliament. Short positions made a bomb. Next month, the tipsheet did it again, with a high street retail chain. Not so much uproar, but subscription slips poured in. 'One day,' said the Shark, 'they're bound to twig that my painstaking company analysis consists simply in looking out for big insider deals. We know who the fiddlers are, we know they're buying tipoffs, and we simply follow their dealings.'

After a few issues – I was well into the new term – all the City pages started using the *International Economic Newsletter* as a heavy source. Sharkey quietened it down after a few coups, but its reputation was made. He also hacked, I don't like to think where from, the next lot of Treasury and economic statistics, which happened to be pretty menacing, and bombed the stockmarket with them. The funniest thing about this exercise was that in spite of Sharkey's interview with Father, and the free subscription, Father never associated Sharkey with *this* newsletter – one of his employees couldn't have the clout to rock the boat on this scale. He asked Sharkey rather patronisingly how his little venture was going, and asked him if he'd seen *I.E.N.*, which was a fine example of the fruits of careful research.

A less funny development was the possible suicide, and probably murder, of Herr Erlenmeyer. Somebody evidently thought he was talking out of turn: Sharkey said that it indicated the kind of people we were dealing with. Rather prudently, he didn't communicate his connection with the tipsheet operation to the Disciples. I only got to hear of it when they wasted Erlenmeyer, who was one of our hooks into Burnside. Sharkey said it was unimportant – we'd used up that particular resource – and Erlenmeyer might serve to justify his, Sharkey's, paranoid attitude towards garrulity.

'Now, David,' he said, 'it's your turn. I want you to call Hatton, Black the brokers, ask for Mr Hatton, and give him your account. I'll feed you enough tips which don't go in the sheet to give you a reputation as a financial smartass, and we take it from there.'

'Take it where to?'

'In due time, you ask Hatton to let you do your dealing on-line into their computer. Hatton thinks he understands hi-tech communications – that's their big selling point here and in America. They lend selected clients an outlet and a modem to play with, and their buy and sell points are automated – if it falls x points they sell to stop loss, if it falls $x + y$ points they buy back in. You'll get a personal entry code – then we'll go in and poke around to assess the possibilities. I need a feed-in point well away from the Firm.'

'And when you do, the shit falls on me,' I said.

'Certainly not. If I can get into their keyword lexicon I'll pick one of the bigger fiddlers and lay the odium on him. Now, you go along like a nice little yuppie and tell Hatton how much you love the Grocer, and how you respect his hi-tech approach. He'll tell you a lot of utter garbage, unless he twigs that you understand computers, in which case he'll eat out of your hand. Now go to it.'

Sure enough, Hatton Black inhabited not the usual pre-Bang mausoleum, but another Paxton greenhouse full of consoles and nubile women – quite enjoyable to visit, if your zero-input relaxation is guessing pubic hair colour – and Hatton himself was a pinstriped Tonton Macoute from Harvard Business School with dark glasses which he wore indoors, pheromone aftershave, and a Croynge accent you could cut with a chainsaw: delighted to see me, certain we'd have a splendid business association, highest regard for my Father's firm, one of the best of the *old* school, though we could ha, ha, show them a thing or two about the communications revolution, and would I like a tour of their dealing facility? I would, and I noticed, as we progressed, several little books of client entry numbers lying about, plus a shelf in the open office full of more little books marked STRICTLY CONFIDENTAL, which looked promising. They had a reasonable mainframe, not as big as the one Sharkey was using, and a lot of on-commission erks glaring at each other and dealing furiously. 'Open-plan office, keeps the staff competitive,' said Hatton, and he pointed out his great

123

invention, a whacking great LED display over each dealer showing the aggregate number of shares he'd shifted since work began. 'If they stay on late we reset it to a non-zero figure for next day,' said Hatton, rubbing his graduation rings. If Father's was Caesar's Palace, this was the Sahara. When one of the damsels tripped in to find Hatton, I appropriated one of the little books, and no alarm bells rang. But when I inspected it in the gent's I found a magstrip in the binding. That went down the loo before we went out to business lunch, and the electronic dog at the door didn't bark.

'Pillocks,' said Sharkey. 'What's to stop anyone copying one? But you did a great job – you've saved me a lot of time. Hatton, my friend, is ripe for picking as and when required.' I told Sarah where I had been, but in view of what happened to Erlenmeyer I thought it wise to censor the account.

With many protestations that he wasn't trying to spend my money, Sharkey insisted that I had to have a new car – and a house. In view of Sarah, I had to agree about the house, though Mansur said glumly, 'Now you are prosperous, you will leave us. It is no fault, I will do the same.' However, there aren't any houses in reach of the College. A henhouse, or a Victorian workman's house, being priced at around £¼M, I decided to stay put. Luckily Mansur knew the landlord, who turned out to be a fellow Sikh, and he sold me the lease, albeit at an inflated price, so I now had the whole house. The bottom flat was vacant because the plumbing had been condemned. Feeling a bit guilty, I set about the process of gentrification, in spite of Sharkey's fears that the address would go down badly with insurers and with Hatton, Black.

As to the car, I bought a Rover, which is the yuppie's stepladder to a Mercedes, but I put the Volkswagen in one of the two sheds in the overgrown garden, after knocking a hole in the rear wall for access: after that we started to dig the garden.

Sharkey's out-of-hours activity on the Firm's computer wasn't all heavy on economics – he accessed, among other things, a gay bulletin-board, and read the expressions of undying affection and the lonely hearts adverts on it. By putting in a retro-probe, he identified the mainframe in Hatton, Black's office as the point of storage, and Hatton himself as the chief poof – which explained why all those little nubiles looked so hungry. He also provided Cynthia with a mailbox (better than notes pinned to doors) because she preferred the up-market, non-violent clientele which was computer literate. She started a very popular scheme whereby she would train a wife/mistress/primary significant person as a birthday present for the man who was screwing them – hopefully it would get less chauvinist when women started getting their males trained: the sales resistance to this seemed to come from the unwillingness of wives to send their husbands to Cynthia – but the list of names was astonishing.

Sharkey, moreover, had one interesting item for the Disciples when we next met. In his excavations he kept running into a concern called Antrochem, pharmaceuticals importer. Antrochem's operations appeared to consist in running a money carousel – large lumps of cash would turn up in one account, then shift to a different bank when a corresponding sum of fresh money came in to top up account number one. They dealt wholly on-line through the international net, and Sharkey put a Trojan Horse in their system: with that, plus Latchkey, he was able to scan all Antrochem's market activities. It had a factory in Tijuana, an office in Detroit, and operated from the Cayman Islands, so you couldn't trace the directors. But the kingpin did have the initials T.R.A.

Sarah and I sat up simultaneously, and said, 'Those are Antrobus's initials – Thomas Rowbottom Antrobus. Could it be?'

Sharkey said the same thing had occurred to him, and it probably was.

'What's he up to, Shark?'

'Well, obviously, laundering.'

'Do we know where he's getting the hot money?'

'I did think of designer drugs,' said Sharkey, 'but I think Antrobus isn't the dope-pushing type: also in Mexico the mob and the police have dealing sewn up, and Antrobus would be scared to muscle in. So I used an Interpol access code and got the Tijuana firm's pharmaceutical licence: they make steroid hormones.'

'Don't tell me Antrobus is flogging virility,' said Sarah.

'It will be athletics,' said Sarkar. 'There is a very big market in gyms for these things – all those people who make their muscles bulge, like this. It is for vanity and attractive to ladies.'

'It is not,' said Violet, 'attractive to ladies. I think they're ridiculous, and so do most women.'

'You know,' said Sarkar, 'some women do it too. And of course athletes, a high proportion of athletes. But it is both harmful and cheating.'

'Antrobus,' said Sharkey, 'appears to have got himself a big slice of the illegal steroid market. Now he didn't have the wit to do that, marketing-wise, unless someone put him up to it, and he didn't have the capital, so he has to have backers. And the backers, though they're under deep cover, with code names, have Swiss account numbers. Those take time to match up, now Erlenmeyer's out of blackmail range, but one of his backers is Hatton and another's the Under-secretary for Health and Social Security via his multipurpose secretary. Another is a bigshot in Customs and Excise. But, as the man said, there is more. The same outfit owns a fish-processing concern in Brixham and three trawlers: bingo. That's evidently the pipeline. The chap behind it all appears to be Joe Nimrod, the shotput gold medallist who got unfrocked, or demedalled, or whatever they do, for doping.'

'So we blow him sky high,' said Violet.

'Why?' said Sharkey. 'I simply gave you this little story to illustrate the power of the method. We are not policemen. We see all and say nothing, until there's something we want. You don't like that, Father Malachi?'

'No, but I agree with it,' said Malachi. 'The Church is under no illusions about human wickedness, Shark, and it usually hears about it in confidence.'

'But doesn't resort to blackmail in the interests of social justice?' said Vi.

'Not as a rule – if you exclude threatening them with Hellfire if they don't shape up,' said Malachi, 'and I take it you're not doing all this out of a perverse love of corruption, Shark: you're moving toward a final come-uppance, right?'

'Like hell I am,' said Sharkey. 'I'm a stand-in for the recording angel. We're going to move the Last Judgment up a bit, preach – into the terrestrial environment. Is that the sin of pride?'

'I don't know,' said Malachi, 'but it'll serve them bloody well right and do them a lot of spiritual good. As far as my ethical position goes, I'd like you to knock the bejasus out of them. God doesn't, which is as well for all of us fallible sinners, but there's nothing to say that you mustn't.'

Malachi sounded in good form, but he buttonholed me afterwards to say he was pretty upset about Matthew. I wasn't too pleased either, since I'd seen him getting into a taxi with Cynthia after several successive classes. My worry wasn't that his vocation had run out, but that the chap might hurt himself badly escaping from the menagerie. Malachi expressed the same concern in other words. I had to point out that Cynthia and Matthew were both adults, and had to make their own choices.

'I wish,' said Malachi, 'he'd talk about it to someone. He's not unique – God made us all with testicles, and some young people take on commitments out of devotional enthusiasm before they know the score. I can handle it, because I'm doing what I want to do – he can't.'

'Well,' I said, 'presumably he talks about it to his confessor.'

'That I very much doubt,' said Malachi. 'You may not see it like that, David, but I think he's a soul in danger.'

'I agree,' I said. 'He's a soul in a self-destructive muddle. But which would sort him out quicker – his instructor, or Cynthia? She's not insensitive, Malachi, nor doing it for kicks. In a sense she's renounced sexuality as much as any nun, and I personally think she understands what's going on. He'll talk to her, won't he?'

Malachi thought about that. Finally he said that perhaps I was right, and that God would look after Matthew one way or another, which struck me as a very broadminded way of looking at it.

A very odd phone call. One of those golden-voiced ladies who try to sell you stock over the phone, telling me that Mister Thorburn was on the line for me: a brief period of muzak, a click, and one of those Big Bang voices asking if it could have lunch with me at the Etoile. I asked it why. It had a proposition it wanted to discuss. I told it I didn't buy stock, invest in hamburger restaurants, or buy insurance, and it would be wasting a lunch. Hearty laughter – it had heard that I was a bit of a humorist, and it could assure me it had nothing like that in mind. In fact, my father had suggested it should approach me.

'Well,' I said, 'in the first place, who exactly are you?'

Brief pause. It expected to be recognised, no doubt. 'I'm Thorburn – you've heard of Thorburn, Mazes and Solomon?'

'Yes,' I said, 'you're company promoters. I thought as much.'

'We're actually,' said the voice, 'financial advisers.'

'I don't need financial advice.'

It did assure me, it wasn't trying to canvas business. It wanted my help with a project.

'I don't invest in projects.'

The voice was a bit exasperated. It didn't want my capital backing, because it had plenty of rich clients, but it did want to discuss something with me.

'Which you can't discuss on the phone?'

'Precisely.'

'Well,' I said, 'ring back in ten minutes. I intend to check you out with my Father.'

Sarah, who heard half of this, said that the caller seemed to have got more than he bargained for. I rang Father. He was a bit evasive – yes, he had suggested Thorburn speak to me – no, he wasn't a tipster but a highly respected City figure, and he, Father, would be obliged if I'd meet the chap. At worst I'd get a good lunch. Accordingly, I gave Thorburn a lunch appointment, and took Sarah with me. Thorburn was a little fellow with a quiff, who looked the accountant and was thoroughly disconcerted to find Sarah there. He told her the business was – er – confidential, and she beamed back and told him she was accustomed to discretion, which she then negatived a little by having lobster cardinale while I had an ascetic salad and told him I didn't drink, to establish a bit of authority, good as the lobster looked.

'What I wanted to discuss with you,' said Thorburn, 'is this. You probably don't know that the Government is making preliminary soundings to privatise the Health Service – that information is, of course, highly confidential.'

'It's also as big as a barn door,' I said. 'Why otherwise would they build new hospitals, decline to staff them, and run the NHS into the ground? They're building up assets to sell off – it's the old Grocer trick over again. Go on.'

'Well,' said Thorburn, 'we are assisting a consortium of clients who intend to become bidders, on a large scale: a very large scale. Now a corporation which takes over health care will of course need very high-powered medical and financial direction, but it will also need a Board which is widely based, and which commands public confidence. It will be a large board, drawn from a representative spectrum of ages and occupations. I am inviting you to join it.'

'You need a philosopher?' I said.

'We're aware of your book on social ethics,' said Thorburn, 'but you do have a name which carries credit in the City, and though you are a man of substance you have no direct commercial involvement. You're also in an under-represented age group.'

'And Father, doubtless for good reasons, didn't want to get mixed up in it, right?'

'Your Father has extensive financial interests. We don't want our Board to be overweighted with City names. You realise that health provision is rather different from the run of purely commercial projects,' said Thorburn.

'I do. Now, who exactly is it that you want the Board to front for? A bunch of Conservative top brass who are steering health care into their pockets?'

'You're being very severe,' said Thorburn.

'Right. Who are they?'

'A bunch of Conservative top brass, who couldn't possibly go public on this operation.'

'Payoff?' I said.

'Sixty thousand a year in director's fees, and you'd have to turn up at meetings.'

'I'd turn up.'

'Do I take it that you accept?'

'Not necessarily,' I said. 'This story would be worth more than sixty thousand in personal satisfaction if I call Labour headquarters.'

'You wouldn't do that. This interview was confidential,' said Thorburn. His face began to sag a little and go plum-coloured.

'Watch me,' I said. 'I haven't signed the Official Secrets Act. How about another sixty G's for not blowing the whistle?'

'Out of the question: a most improper suggestion. But I should add that acceptance of our offer will carry with it an excellent chance of academic prospects. The consortium will be endowing a Chair of Medical Ethics.'

'Which I get?'

'I'm not authorised to promise that – it will rest with the University. But you would have an excellent chance of being recommended by the donors.'

'Is there a deadline?' I asked.

'We want your answer as soon as possible.'

'Of course. I'll give it as soon as the Chair you mention is sewn up – in writing, of course. And in the event that I accept, there will have to be funding for me to engage my wife as my research assistant.' Sarah kicked me under the table.

'Understood.' I told him I'd call him early next week. Sarah asked me if I was seriously thinking of going along with this. In reply I showed her the mini-tape recorder and we went to play the tape to Sharkey.

'What do I do, Shark? Post the tape to the Opposition?'

'No way. You accept, you get the names, you play the virtuous moneygrubber. I'll see the Opposition get tipped off in confidence. The Lord has delivered them into our hand,' said Sharkey. 'Hold it, Sarah: we can do far more damage that way. The Opposition know damn well what's brewing, but they need to know which Tory bigwigs have their hot little hands in the till. If you two keep your mouths shut and play along, they'll think they're safe. You gave Thorburn a bad shock by showing him you disapprove, but they all believe in venality, and when you call him and accept he'll hold a little celebration. Incidentally, your Father's got his head screwed on. He can see this will leak. If it's a big dummy board, one of the little MBE's is bound to talk. Bright of him.'

I did venture to ask Joe Wiston if he thought the Grocer meant to privatise NIH and cut in the Right People. He looked at me as if I were attending his paediatric clinic. 'What else?' he said. 'Have you only just realised that, David?'

'Makes you want to vomit, or commit murder,' I said.

'I've been doing the first quietly for weeks. I'm now meditating the second,' said Joe.

'Doc,' I said, 'we think we can scotch this, so you may not need to. You can do that if we fail. Only don't be surprised at anything you hear about me, whatever it may look like. Sharkey thinks we've got an even chance of doing some real damage.'

The College post contained a letter in a fair round hand which looked as if the writer wrote in circles, like the palmleaf scripts which are designed not to split the leaf. It was familiar, and I had a shrewd idea what the letter would say.

Dear David, I'm sorry about the uproar there will be, and I hope it doesn't damage you or the course. I'm *not* being irresponsible, I took on a professional obligation and I have to see it through. M is both deeply sensual and deeply religious and one or other of these will destroy him if someone doesn't help him put them together. I can do that, because I have sakti skills and can take him through the Curtain. Don't be concerned about either of us – I needed to go away in any case: some of the customers were getting unpleasant, also I've been getting threats. Tell Sharkey I think somebody knows about the Disciples.

Love,

Cynthia.

131

Damnation: not a moment too soon. Malachi on the phone: 'David – is Matthew with you?'

'No.'

'Because we've lost him – he's apparently flipped. Do you know where he is?'

'Not geographically. Apparently he's with Cynthia.'

'She shouldn't have done that,' said Malachi. 'When it comes to an end she'll have spoiled a very good man. I thought she had more decency.'

I told Malachi not to judge her – she seemed to me to be showing extremely good clinical sense. 'Matthew wouldn't have flourished as a priest, he isn't you, Malachi. He'd have been tormented or unedifying or both.'

'Then what is she doing to him?'

'From a letter she just wrote me, teaching him Tantrik yoga.'

'And what the mischief does that mean, David?'

'Learning to use his sensuality in the interests of his spirituality, as I understand it.'

'You're the credulous one, David. I think it's a tragedy. But it's not your fault. You'll let me know if he contacts you? I'm his friend here – the brass will be rough with him.'

Enter Garner, squeaking in panic, and a rotund, rather nice Monsignor who understood the stresses on young ordinands and felt that Matthew needed counselling. I managed to eject Garner. It was pointless to assure the Monsignor that he didn't have the dimmest idea what was going on inside Matthew – he put it down to simple penile insurrection, natural but deplorable – and I didn't mention Cynthia's missionary activities. Of course, said the Monsignor, no blame attached to the course – he personally had sent Matthew and Malachi on it. Garner was hopping about in the corridor, saying that it was desperately unfortunate, could do great harm to the College, and he did feel that I was too anxious to disturb students rather than teach them. Sarah, when I told her the score, said, 'What did you expect? Cynth was too wellbehaved to teach you Tantrik yoga, and here were those two little pink priests – I mean, it must have been irresistible.

I hope she treats him decently; he's burned his boats. You realise that even if they unfrock him he's still a priest?'

'He can't be defused, or disinfected, or whatever they do to them?'

'No – he'll always have the power to turn bread into the body of Christ. He'll find it difficult to escape into another paradigm.'

Cynthia's letter, I noticed, had an Indian stamp on it – postmark Dharamsala, so it looked as if they were with the Tibetans, who might or might not approve of Cynthia's tantrika, but who could certainly talk to Matthew in terms which he'd understand. Clever Cynthia. Sarah was quite upset. She was going to miss Cynthia as a friend and guru.

Instead of holding a postmortem on the paper (Garner's idea) the last class turned into a speculative discussion about the Brahman and the Bohmian implicate reality, started by the physicist the girls called Gonzo, but picked up by Malachi – when someone suggested an implicate would have to be a Subjacent Information-Source (what an expression!) Malachi said, 'Do you mean a logos?' The jargonist said he supposed so. 'Does it think?' said Malachi.

From there we got by degrees into whether Malachi's logos 'had a mind', courtesy of Turing. Whether it *was* Mind, and whether that which has a mind has also to be personal. You see the uncurriculability of this bunch. One of the other physicists suggested that an Implicate would 'become personal' only through Man. Malachi said that this was one implication of his view of incarnation. I'd by this time stopped trying to get the herd back in the stockade. I pointed out that this sounded like something Teilhard had been attempting to say, if Malachi wanted to Catholicise an idea which came from physics – and anyhow the idea that a logos could only be personal when it had generated human personality as a kind of fruit-body wasn't original, it went back to the Zohar: 'The Kabbalist rabbis called it the secret doctrine of the Chariot – God needs a chariot, or a probe, to get inside his creation and do what defines a person, namely conduct a dialogue with

133

Man. So Man is the Merkaba, the chariot.' Well, this was the final class of the term, it could freewheel a bit, but instead of singing Auld Lang Syne when the bell went, argument went on, down the passage, out through the front door and in opposite directions down the street. In other words they were 'doing philosophy' of their own proper motion – mostly kicking notions around rather than applying logical analysis to them: but kicking around is antecedent to football, they had heard (if they had paid attention) how Plato, Spinoza et al. addressed the notions they were kicking around, because that was in the curriculum. I don't know about the rank and file but certainly the physicists there didn't look on the class as a tour of extinct intellectual volcanoes, and they showed a praiseworthy eclecticism: time was when any science student wouldn't have bothered to argue with any proposition which was uttered through a dogcollar, and my little theologians were getting prized open, oyster-fashion, by ideas from mathematics. Socratic it wasn't, but I think he'd have quite enjoyed it, unless Garner put hemlock in his coffee.

13

It was done remarkably neatly, with neither fuss nor publicity. They assembled the front-persons quite informally in a college board-room, white wine and canapés, remote from the sordidness of Spivsville – a clutch of minor academics, a lady novelist, a concerned Liberal peeress, a little fellow with rimless glasses who had known Arthur Koestler and who wrote books about fringe medicine, two rather small-bore canons, both habitual broadcasters, and a lay psychologist, ditto. It was, they were told, their role to speak for the People and preserve the Human Face of the Operation.

Thorburn was keeping out of sight – I'd had an interview with him before I went in and sat near the door (they used an oval, Arthurian-style table to seat the pigeons, giving them a warm feeling of equality and boardmanship).

'I take it,' said Thorburn, 'that you are on? Otherwise you wouldn't be here.' I nodded.

'Good. Now, here's what our laywer has drawn up about the professorship. It's not a binding contract, more a letter of intent.'

I read it (not worth the paper it was typed on, though they'd probably made plans to deliver on it), handed it back, and said it wouldn't be necessary.

'I don't want the professorship. You can't really mix this with academic work. Academia has standards, or it ought to have.'

He gave me a long, hard look.

'Well, that's up to you. We would have liked to have another senior academic ethicist on the Board, in the interest of credibility. I take it you have no objection to accepting the fees we agreed?'

'None whatever,' I said, 'But I'm ready to bet you aren't paying the same rate to all those characters in there, are you?'

'I'll answer that to stop you discussing it with them. The standard director's fee is £2000 per annum. Additional remuneration in the form of extraordinary payments, payment for services, and expenses are on a scale of ...'

'How much you want that name. £2000 plus a slush fund. Why me, Mr Thorburn? Why an under-recognised college lecturer who doesn't appear on the box, hasn't any clout, and sees through the whole scam anyway?'

'Because we want your old man's firm in as backers, and that was his price,' said Thorburn. 'Since you see through what you call the scam, I'm a little surprised you're willing to play. I don't think it's the money.'

I grinned blandly. Thorburn was coming ever so slightly unravelled. 'Because,' I said, 'I wanted to hear your frank opinion of this operation.'

'I'm not paid to give frank opinions of the firm's operations, once they've been adopted,' said Thorburn.

'Then what are you paid for? Aren't you the bull goose in Thorburn, Mazes and Solomon?'

'When you're being leant on by Downing Street, there is no bull goose,' he said.

'Blackmail?' I asked genially.

'Nothing of the kind – simply that when Auntie says march, you march, or you encounter Obstacles,' said Thorburn. 'You're no fool, so don't pretend not to understand.'

'Charming – I understand. Now tell me your frank opinion of the project.'

'The same as yours. It's an utter disgrace, it's corrupt, and it's in flagrant breach of election promises. It's the kind of behaviour that gets Conservatism a bad name: I *am* a Conservative!'

'Naturally.'

'I'm humiliated and disgusted. My elderly aunt has no

means – when she needed a hip replacement, she was told, wait three years, or pay up and we'll do it next week: what sort of a country is this?' He *had* unravelled, he was going a rich plum colour, quite a decent Tory inflamed by what he was seeing of Spivsville. Jesus, I thought, if it's gone that far, among characters like him, there's bound to be a hanging before long – probably when the first big bubble bursts.

'I agree,' I said, 'and that's why I'm joining the board.' I may have misread it, but I think he looked thoroughly relieved – he'd been indiscreet, but indiscreet with the right person.

'Names?' I said.

Thorburn pointed to the telephone, then to the door, then made a throat-cutting motion.

'You think so?'

'Could be. Go along in with the other – pigeons. I'll be in touch,' he said. Very rustily, he actually winked.

After the sales pitch, they had a jolly jabber about ethics, humanising the Health Service, and Moving On towards New Conceptions. That died out in a rattle of egos and privately-crafted dentures and they broke up into the knots one sees at a private view. I headed for the door.

There was a daughter of Spivsville lying in wait with a book. 'Mr Thorburn asked me to give you this,' she said, as if she went with it. I accepted it gravely and took it home. It was a copy of Whitaker, and someone had gone through it with a high-lighting pen. Sarah and I went round with it to Sharkey.

The Disciples were getting thinner on the ground. Cynthia had departed with her priest: Malachi didn't always come – I think his confessor warned him off associating with the class. Violet had stopped coming also – too busy with her under-ground railroad: Violet liked active conspiratorial involve-ment. Sarkar was going to have to go back to India before too long. Sharkey was going to be left with Sarah and me.

'It was my intuition,' said Sharkey, 'that three is the right size for a conspiracy – with a little outside help. We should now set a timetable. At any time, someone might stumble on something. I intend to take the initial steps four weeks from now, and set D-day for eight weeks later.'

137

Sarah wanted to know exactly what he was going to do. Sharkey told her it was highly technical and best kept in one head. 'However,' he said, 'realise that the casino game has changed. Once you had to spread rumours if you wanted to rig it. Now it's fully automatic. All the programs I've entered have stop-loss orders in them which fire automatically. I've been introducing a few more – enough to make sure that when we're ready, any stone that slips will start an avalanche. And all the viruses and crabs I've been spreading strategically will trigger from those stop-loss orders, so that they can't put Humpty Dumpty together again, because their data will go haywire. Run a loop in my brain and I get an epileptic fit. I've designed the computational equivalent. It's quietly asleep on discs all over the City, waiting for the word.'

'They'll spot it and go back to pencil and paper,' I said.

'They won't be able to. The data will alter themselves, and if they try to exchange them they'll exchange viruses. It's very, very pretty.'

'You see,' he continued, 'they've created a virtual world – it's like the video game model of reality we used in the class discussion: it's your model, David. Now suppose one could make magic work – suppose one could manipulate the objective video game. Scientists would commit suicide in droves, rationalism would expire – maybe that will happen – Cynthia thinks so. But whether or not, we *can* alter the Laws of Nature in the Spivsville game – it's manmade and a lot of it bloody badly constructed. Each time they upgrade a ROM they do it around old material, they patch in and patch on – you can make some of the advanced machines regress to infancy and talk the babytalk we programmed in years ago if you know where the fossils are buried – now and then they do it spontaneously, and most programmers can't for the life of them figure what went wrong. Imagine a wizard who could make gravity reverse sense – it would demolish the Universe. We can do that to the Spivsville game, and they'll never know what hit them.'

'Computer magic, dirty trick, or both?' I said.

'Oh, both, as indicated.'

'Won't they interfere? I mean, if yuppies are jumping out of

City windows, who's going to worry if the Minister for Reproduction slept with an Alsatian dog?'

'Timing,' said Sharkey. 'Crashed yuppies are going to be looking for a scapegoat. Incidentally, I picked up an interesting memo – off an open free-enterprise billboard too. It's the counterpart of your raid on health care, it's called Amenity Housing, and it's buying up Council estates; but look who's putting up the cash – Antrochem International.'

'Laundry.'

'The perfect one. Antrobus comes back from Ibiza, kisses the Grocer's hand, or some other anatomical feature, gets a safe by-election seat and a knighthood, and enjoys himself as an officially-sponsored slum landlord – all on pushing steroids.'

'Did you say Antrochem?' said Sarkar. He'd been sunk in a beanbag chair, going through Sharkey's printouts.

'I did – do they mean something to you?'

'Only my brother – he's a merchant captain – his last ship was under charter to Antrochem.'

'What route?' said Sharkey.

'India-Mexico-Liverpool I believe. Sometimes he would stop in Britain on the India-Mexico leg. Probably when I go home, I will go on his ship – no need for air fare.'

'That,' said Sharkey, 'is charming. You don't by any chance know what's on the manifest, do you?'

'It is agricultural chemicals and sow farrowing equipment,' said Sarkar. 'But my brother was unhappy.'

'Well, the agricultural chemicals will be opium one way and steroids the other,' said Sharkey. 'Antrobus is too smart to run hard drugs into Britain – probably subcontracts to the Mob in exchange for territory. And I imagine the sow farrowing equipment was Kalashnikovs or similar. Your brother was dead right to get out. What's his present ship carrying?'

'Oh, palm oil one way, grain the other,' said Sarkar. 'He'll be in port here next week.'

'What about his former ship?'

'The *Orient Emerald*: still trading,' said Sarkar.

'I'll bet she is. Shark, can we get Antrobus, just as a sideline?' I asked.

'It's tempting,' said Sharkey, 'but let us keep the main

139

project in view. Sarkar, you and David prepare a position paper on Antrobus. We'll send it to the Press, the Opposition, the Drugs Squad, the Fraud Squad, and the Prime Minister. At a suitable opportunity. Give you something to do while I get on with the main business.'

'It will not involve my brother?' said Sarkar. 'Otherwise I would have said nothing.'

'No way – he's an upright citizen who suspected some monkey business and exposed it,' said Sharkey. 'He should get a pat on the back.'

'Or a knife in the back when Antrobus hears he shopped him,' said Sarkar.

'We'll keep him entirely out of it,' I said. 'It'll be nice to take a smack at some of them – for starters.'

Sarah, Sarkar and I prepared the Antrobus file, starting with Amenity Housing PLC, through Antrochem and its trading activities, down to Antrobus's raid on Father – all purely factual: Sharkey duplicated it, on the Institute for Personal Information letterhead, and Sarah and I took it down and posted the copies, full glove precautions, from Hastings. Then there was silence in heaven for the space of, well, far too long: each recipient, including the investigative Press, knew who else had had it from the appended circulation list. They were talking about it in Fleet Street, but the buzz was that the Home Secretary had asked for discretion, so as not to interfere with a Drugs Squad operation. Eventually the *Orient Emerald* docked. There was a highly-publicised drugs raid and a lot of hash was exhibited to the Press. No steroids, no mention of Antrobus, not good enough. The Institute sent a personal dossier to an independent television producer – but it was going to take some time for the cover-up to be punctured. What did appear in print was a story that the Government were extremely keen to interview the Institute for Personal Information. Sharkey was horribly didactic about this operation: we'd attracted attention to ourselves, but Antrobus was being protected from on high – what did we expect?

140

Then the first shot in Sharkey's own strategic plan arrived. The latest *International Economic Newsletter* dropped through my letterbox. It carried a remarkable editorial.

The editors of this newsletter have a responsibility to their readers. They are fully aware that if they offer a 'sell' recommendation, on the basis of a detailed study of company prospects, the shares of that company will suffer as a result, and the prediction, to that extent, be self-fulfilling. The alternative would be to suppress adverse comment: such reticence would only postpone the fall in share prices, not avoid it, and our readers pay for sound information.

We face a far more difficult situation in regard to matters which affect not a company but the national economy. General favourable or unfavourable predictions are part of a general tide of comment. But what is our responsibility in regard to *specific* information likely to affect sterling? National prosperity is a concern for all British investors. There would be a strong argument for preserving confidentiality in regard to any information likely to produce serious damage – certainly if it were in any sense speculative, but equally if it were undoubtedly authentic. Impending Budget changes, impending revaluation, and many other pieces of financial or policy information could be highly damaging if made public. The legal position is unclear – it is not at all certain whether these items are 'official secrets' only if obtained improperly from official sources, or whether the same would apply to the results of informed deduction from lawfully available material – the only source which our analysts employ in this Newsletter.

We have seriously considered these issues, and have come to the conclusion that reticence is not the answer. A financial bulletin should not make deliberate mischief, or talk down either a currency or a company from improper motives. But if from legitimate analysis, which our subscribers pay us to perform, we reach conclusions which may, when published, cause adverse effects on the National economy, those subscribers are entitled to share the results of our study. An economy which can only be propped up by reticence is already in a vulnerable position, and investors who believe it to be strong are being deceived.

On this basis, and in full awareness that we may incur criticism, we intend to devote the whole of our next issue to the position of sterling and the soundness of its present support mechanisms ...

And so on. This was vintage Sharkey – it would cause the maximum jitters with the minimum information: there would be intense Treasury activity to stop it, but the *Newsletter* was being produced, I am not quite sure how, in Amsterdam and edited by a fictitious Dutchman. I hoped Sharkey had covered his tracks efficiently. He'd have the palace eunuchs running in circles screaming for MI5 to find out what the *Newsletter* had got hold of. Sharkey grinned broadly when asked. 'Nothing. The next issue will say that after mature consideration, we've decided not to risk publishing official secrets, and we'll limit our comment to buy-sell-hold advice. Our advice regarding sterling is – SELL. Riadh's been trying to phone our Amsterdam office. This is the pebble to start the avalanche – right?'

I was in bed re-reading this diabolical piece of guile when the doorbell rang – I thought briefly of the Special Branch, but Sarah had already gone to answer it. She came back.

'It's your Violet,' she said.

'She's not my Violet. What does she want?'

Last time it had been the other way about.

Violet out of breath, apologetic, 'I'll leave you,' said Sarah, 'to it.'

'No, Sarah, chuck it – you've both got to hear this. It's business. I need advice.'

I sat up, Sarah sat down, and Violet boiled over. She'd been trying to smuggle in some Salvadorians. Two men had called on her. 'They knew all about it, and they were obviously spooks of some kind. They asked me if I knew I could be sent to prison. Then they said they'd cooperate with me if I'd cooperate with them: they'd arrange for the admission of some of my clients, but I'd have to pay with information about the whole refugee support organisation – who was in it, how it operated, and when it was planning a move. I said I'd think it over. What do I tell them?'

We told her to hold her horses until she heard from Sharkey, and stay away from the Disciples. For all we knew she'd been tailed to my place. I called Sharkey from a phone box, and we convened to discuss what to do with her.

Sharkey said, 'Jesus wept – I expected this. We've got to get rid of her.'

'We can't dump her in the Thames,' said Sarah. Sarkar looked profoundly shocked.

'No, but we're going to have to tell her to play along. She knows far too much about Operation Spivsville, and about the Institute, *and* her current boyfriend is mixed up with the Palestinians and the INLA: she's accident-prone and she's a menace.'

'So?'

Sharkey was cloudcapped for about ten minutes. Then he said, 'Sarah – go down, find a phone box which works, call Vi and tell her to play along but stay away from past acquaintances. Tell her it's her civic duty – the authorities may know more than she does, and so on. Be fulsome for the phone tap, and don't give your name, of course.'

'I can handle it,' said Sarah. 'I hope she doesn't blurt.'

'We've got to risk it. Now, Sarkar, did you say your brother was in port?'

'Yes, he's at Southampton,' said Sarkar.

'Sailing when?'

'The day after tomorrow, for Antofagasta.'

'Right,' said Sharkey. 'Now, David, you've got some Indian friends – would that Sikh chap cooperate and keep his mouth shut?'

'Who, Mansur?' I said. 'He'd do anything I asked him. But I'll only ask if it's kosher.'

'It's kosher. He's to see Violet and tell her there are three desperate stowaways on ... what's the ship's name, Sarkar?'

'The *Rajkumar*.'

'The *Rajkumar*, at Southampton, and for the love of Allah ...'

'Mansur's a Sikh, not a Muslim,' I said.

'For the love of the guru sahib, then, she has to go down and see them, pronto. Sarkar, is your brother on a landline?'

Sarah came back. 'I've got her on hold,' she said. 'She actually played it quite well, and called me Mary – we did a sisters act. Now what?'

'We're going to export her if we can,' said Sharkey. 'David,

143

you go back and talk to Mansur.'

I was absolutely frank with Mansur, I owed it him. Mansur adjusted his turban. 'You are wanting me to inveigle a woman on board a ship and export her? Your former fiancée? Is she being a nuisance?'

'She wasn't my fiancée,' I said, 'and she's being pumped by the fuzz about helping refugees. We simply want to get her out of the country for a bit.'

'Only you I would believe about this, David. It sounds like monkey's business in a big way. But you are truthful. What exactly do I tell her?'

I told him, exactly, gave him his return fare, which he tried to refuse, and told him to take her down to Southampton and see her on board the *Rajkumar*.

'If she is suspicious and won't go?'

'Use your own judgment. But we're going to phone her and tell her you're for real. Now, off you go.'

'I hope,' said Sarah, 'that she does go.'

'Still jealous?'

'No, but you did live with her, and I prefer it if she isn't hanging around.'

'Violet,' I said, 'was never serious competition. In the first place she didn't love me. In the second, she couldn't hold a candle to you, Sarah.' I was going to say she was all pubis and no padding, but Sarah wasn't in the mood for male chauvinist jokes. I kissed her instead.

We were actually still in bed, winding down, when Mansur knocked next day. I put on a dressing-gown.

'The *Rajkumar* has sailed,' he said.

'With the lady on it?'

'I did not see her come off, and there was only one gangway. Also it sailed very quietly. I had told her not to worry if the ship moved – they were changing moorings because the Immigration were giving them problems,' said Mansur.

'You,' I said, 'are indeed the descendant of kings. Stay to breakfast.' I got it, pulled Sarah out of bed, and we ate together – Mansur a little uncomfortable at our déshabille, but what could one expect from the English?

144

14

'That man,' said my Father, 'is something of a genius. You may not want to join us, David, but at least I think we owe you for John Sharkey. None of our competitors have a programmer who can touch him.'

'He's good,' I said. 'Probably comes of studying philosophy. It's an excellent discipline for computer people.'

'I wouldn't know,' said Father, 'but I do know that all our competitors have been tying themselves in knots and blaming the machines. They have service people from the makers in permanent residence – whereas Sharkey had our system up and running in a matter of days. Works an enormous amount of unpaid overtime, too.'

I knew what he was working at. I even had a pang of conscience about Father. On Sharkey's instructions I'd moved my money to a Danish bank in Switzerland. Perhaps Sharkey could fix up something to protect Father from the wrath to come: it seemed only fair.

Actually about that time the overtime stopped. The Shark didn't need to be physically present with the mainframe – he could sit at home with a green-glass shaded standard lamp and a PC plus modem, operating by remote control. He could have been a Victorian writing a novel. Occasionally I watched him: all his resources were in place, and he was quietly checking round to make sure his coverage was complete. There was one big City computer which was giving him trouble.

'It's not that I can't get *in*,' he said, 'but when I'm in, things seem to go round in circles. It's like judo.'

I looked over his shoulder.

'I think,' he said, 'there may be a Trojan Horse in here already, and if so it isn't mine. Try again.'

The little frantic square on the screen started to write: ENTER YOUR PASSWORD.

'Whoops,' said Sharkey, 'that shouldn't be there. It's illicit. Wish I knew who's playing silly buggers.'

'A hacker? A business competitor?'

'Could be.'

'Which system is it?'

'Your pal Hatton – and you saved me a lot of work by nicking their code book. I'm trying to make up my mind if they're being hacked by amateurs, or if they've got a bloody original programmer ... Jesus!'

'What's wrong?'

'A wizard recognises a wizard. Hamsen.'

'You said he was retired.'

'But not dead. I'm just going to try something ...,' he punched away at the keyboard, 'now ... oh my God!'

The little spot had written: SHARKEY, I'M SURPRISED AT YOU. We sat and looked at it.

'Not only did he program this,' said Sharkey, 'he knew I was breaking into it, or he knew I was going to break into it, and he put that answer in! Now, which side is he on?'

'Ask him,' I said. 'He might guess you'd ask that, and he might have put in an answer. Try it.'

Sharkey, after a bit of hesitation, typed in: HAMSEN, WHOSE SIDE ARE YOU ON?

Pause. Then: THE SIDE OF LUCIDITY. DO WHAT YOU MUST. YOU CAN'T DO IT TO THIS SYSTEM, BE WARNED, HAMSEN.

'That sounds like, he won't interfere, but he won't let you tinker with his system.'

'Hamsen all over. But it means there's a major City source I can't touch. It could spoil everything, and make Hatton the biggest shot in the business, because he won't be fooled. Let me think.'

I did. Finally Sharkey said, 'Right. I hate doing this, and I hate it most because Hamsen will know who did it. I'm going to phone Sarkar.'

When Sarkar answered, Sharkey asked him if he could get hold of some fine carbon fibre. Sarkar said he'd try – the engineering department had some, he thought: they'd been working on carbon fibres a while back.

'Submicro strands?' said Sharkey.

'I'll see.'

'What was that about?' I asked.

'On D-day, we've got to knock that mainframe out,' said Sharkey. 'Carbon fibres in the air poison computers – they conduct and cause shorts. That's why they keep the frame in a dust-free atmsophere. And they take time to work, so we go as soon as we can.'

'How do you reckon to get in there?'

'I don't: you're going to. Didn't Hatton take you in there once before? Well, he's going to have to do it again. Tell him you were fascinated.'

'And start chucking powder around?' I said.

'You don't need to. It won't be visible. Just a bag in your trouser pocket and a tube down your trouser leg. The stuff flows nicely if it's fine. And we move D-day up to ten days later. Hatton's system should be on the blink by then, God willing.'

'Which Hamsen will immediately detect.'

'And will be able to do bugger all about. It won't be a question of one error – there should be dozens of intermittent faults. They'll have to scrap that mainframe. You can't clean it up. Fibres stick, and you can't see them.'

'Hamsen will be so mad he'll shop you,' I said.

'They may not believe him,' said Sharkey, 'and by then the City will have enough on its plate. But if I send you a message "Scoot", you scoot. Where will you go, in that event?'

'Ibiza?'

'Extradition treaty. Try Ireland. They don't seem keen on extraditing people there, and you won't need passports, you or Sarah. Book a holiday, just in case, if you're wise.'

147

'Just how much will you need to do, I mean on D-day?' I said.

'I shall latch into the automated clearing system and put in three successive sterling quotations, two-wayed to Frankfurt, Zurich, Tokyo and New York,' said Sharkey. 'The rest will follow. Don't forget, the *Newsletter* will have come out three days earlier.'

'Saying?'

'Saying we've thought better of giving information which might violate the Official Secrets Act, and we will simply give our buy-hold-sell recommendations. Our advice on sterling is SELL WITHOUT DELAY. Riadh and Tokyo dealers please copy, because they will.'

'The Bank of England will buy, surely?'

'It will. *But its computer won't,*' said Sharkey. 'And a great deal of our reserves will be transferred by wire to the Swiss account of one Antrochem Enterprises. I told you it was theoretically possible to drain the UK of currency within minutes.'

'Won't that send sterling up rather than down?' I said.

'It'll cause chaos. The City isn't geared to contradictory signals.'

'What do you expect?'

'Anything could happen. The Government will probably stop all trading in London. But they can't stop the other exchanges, and there'll be a mad rush out of sterling, and possibly dollars as well if the scare is bad enough. One can never predict what Gadarene swine will do when they start running. Now, go home, get an appointment with Hatton, and I'll chase Sarkar. I may have to go elsewhere if he can't deliver.'

In fact, he couldn't. But Sharkey called the manufacturers and asked for some samples. He came clean – carbon fibres presented a hazard of computer sabotage, and he wanted to see how PCB's could be protected and if necessary cleansed. They were most cooperative, and sent round a tin of silvery powder. It came to Father's casino and Sharkey took it home in his briefcase. Sarah looked at me as if I was going to the

148

front at Passchendaele and expressed doubts about the wisdom of this whole thing. I agreed with her, and booked a nice double room at Buswell's, followed by another at the old Railway Hotel in Sligo. I reckoned we'd need a break in any event.

D minus ten. Hatton was delighted to see me, tried to sell me a lot of stock, and was flattered at my interest in the fine modernity of his system. Yes, it was quite the most advanced in the City, and they'd been uncommonly fortunate – they'd secured the most eminent computer authority in the world, and he'd come out of retirement to tackle the challenge. 'It's inviolable, unhackable, proof against computer fraud,' he said 'which is more than one can say for any other system. Including your Father's. That's good, but it isn't truly secure. Dr Hamsen says so.'

'Could he hack into it?' I asked.

'I imagine,' said Hatton, 'that he could. Ours is even protected against radio pickup from outside the building. Only military and Secret Service systems take that sort of trouble.'

'Do let me walk round it again,' I said. 'It's impressive, even to a layman. It reminds me of a tour of the human brain.'

Hatton said I was always the philosopher, and we walked through the avenue of gray filing-cabinet boxes. Fine silver dust falling out of my trouser leg was quite invisible when I looked down. I thanked him, promised some buying orders and went home to Sarah. I think she was amazed I hadn't been arrested.

And the day before D-day I bloody nearly was. I was just turning into the street next to mine when I saw a skidderation. There were three yobs, and in the middle was the little Indian herbalist, taking a beating. I drove straight at the outer yob and knocked him flat against a railing. At that moment Mansur and a couple of other Sikhs came round the corner at a run. Yob Two ran one way, Yob Three the other. All the Sikhs went after Yob Two, the one they saw – I jumped out and chased the other, round the corner, down some steps into a yard, into a doorway. The yob tried to open the door and couldn't, so he turned to face me. From the pink skin on his hand and down the side of his face, I reckoned he was one of the National Front bunch whose lives I'd unintentionally saved, and he had a Stanley knife. He grinned at me, because he saw I didn't have one. For my part, I ostentatiously clenched my left fist, while with my right hand I scratched the right side of my head, hoping he wouldn't see me measuring the distance between his eyeballs to fit my index and fourth finger. He didn't. Instead he held up the Stanley knife. I had to beat his blink reflex, and I would only get one go, but he was watching that fist, and the right-handed swordthrust was the last thing he expected. I felt eyeball, on the right at least, and the yell told me I'd registered. The Stanley knife went skittering, the yob yelled 'Oh, God!' and clapped his hands to his face, so that he wasn't even watching the shin kick which caught him already doubled up. I reckoned that was enough for now and left him.

The Sikhs had not only caught Yob Two and left him in an interesting condition – Mansur had driven my car off the pavement and parked it neatly. The damage had been to the yob it had hit, not to the bumper, but Mansur had polished that. He got in and we drove off – at which point we heard the forces of law and order approaching, but Mansur ducked out of sight and the patrol car didn't bother a white man.

'You got the third one?' said Mansur.

I nodded.

'You didn't kill him, I hope?'

'No, I burst an eyeball – I hope.'

'And you broke the second one's legs,' said Mansur. 'We threw him in the area. They will find him. We were following them discreetly – you should not have joined in.'

'What did you want me to do – let them kill the toubib? I didn't know your posse was on the way,' I said.

'They will tell the police that wicked Asians attacked them,' said Mansur, 'and the police will believe them. You better drop me at the tube station. I think I will be staying with friends for a bit. You will please tell my wife all is well and I have been away since Friday?'

What worried me is that someone might have seen the car number. Mansur said, 'It is all right – everyone in that street is Asian or Afro. Nobody will have seen the car but everyone will have seen the attack on the old man. Not to worry.'

I didn't. I was delighted they were giving the Spivsville Militia a bit of their own medicine, because the Government wasn't going to do it.

In contrast to what happened after the Roys were burned out, the place filled with coppers. The chap who came to see us, Oggie's successor, was quite frank about the enquiries.

'We've taken a statement from the Indian who was attacked, and we know these beauties by heart,' he said, 'but the Chief's terribly worried about vigilante activity. If the Asians take the law into their own hands there could be bad trouble. You don't know of any vigilante activity, do you, Sir?'

I told him I didn't, and I was dead surprised there wasn't any. Furthermore if the police didn't do something about attacks on immigrants, immigrants would have to.

'We're doing our best,' he said, 'but we're undermanned. You know that.'

'I take it the yobs will be charged?'

'When they get out of hospital,' said the policeman, 'and the people who maimed them. Two with fractures and one with a detached retina.'

'Good,' I said, 'if I'd been there, they'd have attacked their next immigrant from wheelchairs.' The policeman looked serious, and when he'd gone Sarah told me my mouth was too big. Anyhow, nobody was arrested – there would have been riots if they had been, and the police knew it – and next day we were going to Sharkey's to watch the button-pressing ceremony.

'Do you think it'll work?' said Sarah.

'God knows. Anything could happen. My guess is that the Occupying Power will rally round and save its skin – after a bit of kerfuffle,' I said.

'I'm getting to feel,' she said, 'that it's all totally unreal.'

151

'Sharkey's effort?'

'And everything else. England coming apart at the seams. The fact that they actually elected those people.'

'They didn't. Forty per cent did.'

'And the way everything's running backwards.'

'I know. I watched the Nuremberg Rally at Blackpool on television. For Jews and non-Aryans read local councillors. We've got nutters running the show. So did the Germans.'

'That was before I was born,' she said. 'Before I was born this time.'

'What?'

'I used to dream a lot about being a child, and being taken away at night by people who smashed up the house. It was horrible. Cynthia explained to me.'

'Explained what?' I said.

'That I'd probably been killed somewhere in Europe. It doesn't frighten me now, not since I talked to her.'

'Cynthia thinks you're a jatismara? That you've been bugged by incomplete depletion?'

'Well, it makes sense. Why do you think I let your father do what he did? I needed security,' she said.

'Which you've now got, I hope.'

'Well, yes, provided you don't get sent down. And history doesn't repeat itself.'

I couldn't offer guarantees on either. There was a risk that if Sharkey's plot came off the Occupying Power would go fascist out of desperation, but we had to do something and we were doing it — meanwhile the best thing to do was to make love, which felt safe at least. Sarah agreed.

After the button pressing, we were going for a holiday in Ireland, without waiting for orders from Sharkey.

We packed the Volkswagen, locked up the premises, wondering whether I'd be back next term and whether there would be a class to come back to, paid our respects to Mrs Mansur, and drove over to Sharkey's. The mood was low key. As soon as the market closed for the day, Sharkey — inevitably — said a few words, to the effect that it might well be that history would remember us even if it didn't know our names. I

152

told him that the IRA let off bombs first and make speeches, if at all, afterwards, and he should bloody get on with it if he was serious.

Sharkey said, 'I take it we are all agreed that we make the attempt?' Sarastro getting ready to squelch the Queen of the Night.

'I have had considerable reservations,' said Malachi, 'but I've overcome them.' Sharkey asked him if he'd like to say a few words of prayer. Sarah giggled, and Sarkar put on his field anthropology look. Malachi said, 'Lord, of thy mercy forgive us if we are in error and prosper us if we do well. Amen.'

Well,

> first he went to make his peace
>   with good old Father Carr
> then he went an' blew the barracks up
>   an' wrecked half Mullingar.

Clearly there were precedents. Sharkey said, 'It'll take a minute or two,' and started typing into his console. A police car went past outside. Sharkey said, 'It's ready to go. One keystroke will release the golem. Who wants the privilege?'

'Punch it yourself and stop being theatrical, Shark,' I said, and he did so.

'Jacta est alea. Anyone want a sandwich?' he said.

'Funny,' said Sarkar. 'This began, did it not, as a philosophy class? That is very far away from computer hacking. You see a connection, David?'

'With moral philosophy, yes: the philosopher as intervener. The Greeks would have liked it. And it's got a certain amount to do with what we said about virtual worlds, hasn't it?'

Sarkar didn't look satisfied. I told the Shark we had to get going to catch the ferry, and said goodbye to Malachi.

'Give me news of Matthew, if he contacts you,' I said.

'I doubt he will,' said Malachi.

I was steering Sarah towards the door when someone started to come up the stairs – or rather to stamp up them: it could have been a bipedal bull elephant. Then the door flew

153

open, and in the doorframe stood a small, elderly man with glaring blue eyes, red face, red beard, nondescript hat rammed down on his head – the general air of an enraged garden gnome. 'Sharkey! I want to talk to you!' it said. 'You others *out*!' And the gnome bore down on Sharkey, who got the table between them. He was as white as a sheet. This had to be Hamsen – Sharkey had been rumbled by the Wizard of Oz. Malachi, Sarkar, Sarah and I met at the bottom of the stairs.

'Who is that?' said Malachi.

'Sharkey's old teacher,' I said. 'He's the king of all computer boffins, and he knows what Sharkey's been doing.'

'He will stop it?' said Sarkar.

'Your guess is as good as mine, doc. We have to go, but we'll hold back a little and see how long he stays.'

In fact, he stayed only twenty minutes. We could hear a mutter of voices, but no content. Finally stump, stump, stump down the stairs and out.

Sharkey was postoperative but recovering. 'He knows it all – knew most of it already, because he's been hacking me. Even congratulated me on some of the subprograms I've been planting.'

'Does he approve?' said Malachi.

'In his odd way, yes – he won't intervene. But he's furious about the carbon fibres. Says it was un-lucid – like resorting to assassination in a chess game: I should have pitted my wits with his, head-on.'

'Did you calm him down?' I said.

'I think so. I told him I knew I was no match – and we couldn't leave one system unfixed, it would let the buggers off the hook. I said, this one's for Turing – in future, they'll treat computer experts with a bit more respect. He huffed a bit, shook hands, and said the next few days would show whether I was as clever as I thought I was. He's going to sit back and watch. He moved Hatton out of sterling as soon as he rumbled what I was doing. He'd pinpointed me when I started doing the same for your Father, David. And he read back my entire strategy to me – he's entered every system in London by the sound of it, just looking and watching.'

154

'He's on our side?' said Sarkar.

'No – on the side of computer science. What tipped him was the way the Grocer cancelled research contracts and shut down academic departments – believes it to be national suicide, so the men of wisdom have to act. Wished us well in a grudging kind of way.'

'No danger there?' I said.

'None. And Hamsen never peached in his life.'

I told Sharkey we'd better be going. We went through the City – still buzzing away, like an insect that's been sprayed and doesn't know it yet. It hadn't started to run in circles or have convulsions. Going West on the motorway, Sarah insisted on getting a news bulletin – all quiet, the Grocer marching round one of the devastated cities making triumphalist noises about a new yacht marina and the conversion of council dwellings into high-priced town houses, car bomb in Lebanon, an MP fined for some kind of fiddle. At the very end, surprising weakness of sterling. So we pressed on, making up time, and only when we rumbled onto the ferry, and the ferry set sail, did Sarah unwind.

15

At Buswell's we turned straight in, kissed and went to sleep. Next morning we made love so long we missed the news and nearly missed breakfast. Then we set out driving West through the much-excavated streets of Dublin, and on into smiling, Grocerless Ireland, leaving the musty smell of the witch's castle a long way behind, listening to Irish radio, eating at a pub and talking to sane people, and coming in good time to the hotel in Sligo with its Victorian glass partitions and its afternoon tea. The chap on the desk signed us in. Then he said, 'That's a terrible business.'

'What is?'

'The crisis you have in England. They said on the news that the English pound's destroyed.'

'We've got dollars,' I said. 'I hope it doesn't hit the Irish punt as well.'

'The news says they have it secured,' said the clerk. 'They probably saw it coming. Here's your key. Will you want a hand up with those bags? Wait while I call someone.'

The character who carried the bags was more communicative. 'It was on the television,' he said. 'It seems the Arabs is pulling out their money from England. You have the Cabinet meeting to stop them.'

'In that case,' I said, 'let's hope they reinvest it in the Republic.'

By common consent neither of us put on the television to see what mischief Sharkey had accomplished. That belonged to another manifold. Probably there would be a few days of uproar and the Grocer would broadcast to the nation and blame Brent Council, and all would be as it was – as if we cared. We drove down the empty beach road at Strandhill – no tourists at this time of year – and sat, wrapped up against the wind, watching the squalls coming in, and the great rock beasts that recline on all sides of Sligo Bay, and Queen Meadhbh's cenotaph on Knocknarea.

'Why didn't we come here before?' said Sarah.

'Well, it belongs to the Irish, and we can't all live here. They cleared out the Occupying Power some time back, and it's up to us to do the same for ourselves,' I said.

'The things you were discussing in the Class,' said Sarah, '*there*, they're ideas. Here, you can feel them coming out of the ground.'

'I know what you mean,' I said. 'There's a large chunk of the Implicate buried somewhere hereabouts, and it makes a hot spot. The Irish use it for poetry. I can see Leibnitz and Spinoza shaking hands and simply listening to it. Has the same effect Mount Kailash had on Hindu philosophers – it's a place for seeing, not thinking.'

'Well,' said Sarah, 'ordinary people live here, and they don't all turn into philosophers.'

'Probably don't need to – the hills do it for them.'

'I don't remember you being turned on by landscapes,' said Sarah. 'It's usually by ideas, isn't it?' She was right: England's incredibly beautiful still, but even a de-Grocerised England doesn't speak answers to fundamental questions under its breath. There *are* experiential hot spots – probably different for different people: Malachi might be tuned-in to Jerusalem or Lourdes. For yours truly it's Varanasi or County Sligo. In the Middle Ages there was one at Walsingham. I suppose that natural philosophy could use pilgrimage in the way that marine biologists use skin diving – to see for themselves. One could hardly put that in the course, however.

There were two figures walking on the beach, their outlines jumping about in the movement of the air as if we were using a long lens. The closer they got, the more they seemed familiar. Sarah pointed without speaking. Sharkey, with a

158

ruinous unbuttoned trench coat which blew, and with him a garden gnome. Sharkey and Professor Hamsen. As if they expected to find us here. Hamsen politely raised his hat.

'The top of the – afternoon – to you,' said Sharkey. 'Can we get in?' I opened the door, letting in the wind, and tilted the seat.

'Well?' I said, 'Satisfied?'

'It'll take a day or two,' said Sharkey. 'The Stock Exchange Council suspended all dealings when they realised the whole information system had gone mad, but they can't stop it – the other exchanges are still open.'

'Has he actually done more than stop dealings for a week?' I said to Hamsen.

'Sharkey has started an avalanche,' said Hamsen, 'which is what he intended. Whether the Banks can stop it internationally is another question. I don't see them getting the pound back on its feet. They'll probably go into the European monetary arrangement, if the experts manage to overrule the palace eunuchs, but this man's plan, which he's explained to me now, was admirable. I'm proud of him.'

'The Prof says I'm a patriotic terrorist,' said Sharkey, 'which was what I intended.'

Sarah said that she could see that it was patriotic to bedevil the Grocerites, but wouldn't it do enormous damage to ordinary people?

'Dr Sharkey has performed surgery in the most humane manner possible,' said Hamsen. 'By concentrating his attack on currency, he's burst the bubble which would have burst on its own. A controlled explosion is far less destructive. If he has succeeded, foreign oil and foreign imports will be priced out. We shall have to produce our own. Our exports become unusually cheap. The damage is too big to reverse by jacking up interest. We can't buy American weapon systems. Spivsville has broken its mainspring.'

'Are you an economist?' I said.

'No – don't trust them, either. If I'm wrong, the proof of the pudding will be in the eating. I don't think we shall see another triumphalist Tory conference – unless it's based on

159

Dunkirk, self-reliance, apple pie and Mother. They could change gear – any politician can chamaeleonise. But I think the Queen Wasp is dead. Will you drive us back to Sligo?'

'You'll have dinner with us?' I said. 'All the conspirators?'

'No,' said Sharkey, 'we've got an invitation. We'll be staying with Cynthia and Matthew.'

'They're *here*?'

'They have a cottage at Grange. They're also married. And keeping a low profile in view of their history, in case the Church locates them. They aim to start a small community. And we may well be working with them,' said Hamsen.

'Working?'

'We're obtaining premises for a small institute to work on AI,' said Sharkey. 'The objective is to examine non-Kantian modes of data processing – demonics, you called it, David: learning to think like little green men, or yogis.'

'What about Father?'

'I resigned two weeks ago. He thinks I was headhunted by Logica, and I let him believe it.'

'Who's funding this? Not HM Government?'

'Not bloody likely, not this lot. NASA gave us a contract to discover ways of talking to extraterrestrials – not much, but it's in dollars. The Japanese industry is interested. And we have a bottomless grant from a benefactor, haven't we?'

'We have,' said Hamsen, 'its name is Antrochem Industries.'

'That,' I said, 'is a bit near the bone.'

'Well, any large subvention these days comes from crooks of one kind or another,' said Hamsen, 'better Antrochem than Star Wars. The Irish Government insists that we don't involve ourselves in military contracts, and I agree with them.'

'Dr Hamsen was told by the Americans he could name his figure if he'd go on record that SDI would work, and double if he'd make it work,' said Sharkey. 'That's why he took out Irish nationality and settled here: safer than Grocerland – there, they'd have tried to frame him.'

'Moreover,' said Hamsen, 'we would welcome additional logicians and philosophers as recruits to our staff, Dr Knight. I am deeply influenced by Dr Sharkey's recommendation.'

'That's up to Sarah,' I said. 'She has a job too. What happens when they catch up with Antrobus?'

'Nothing,' said Sharkey. 'In the first place, the charitable fund is irrevocable: Antrobus wants fire insurance. And in the second place, he's a very big donor to Tory funds. In fact, some of 'em think he rigged this sterling business – he's known to be miffed that he's paid for a peerage and didn't get one.'

'I think,' said Sarah, 'David can write to Mr Garner. And I'll write to the Board of City Morals. It doesn't sound as if they'll need me. Can't we all have dinner with Cynthia?'

Hamsen mumbled something about Sarah being better off in something more lucid, and we headed for Grange.

They were stirring days. Matthew looked positively chubby. Smoke could still be seen rising from London and was visible in Dublin. After about three weeks, when it cleared, most of Spivsville was owned by the Japanese – and, it turned out, by my Father, thanks to Sharkey's precautions. I got two letters.

Dear David,

We were all deeply sorry to receive your letter of resignation, not least I myself. I do, however, fully understand your wish to engage in such a stimulating project, even though I do not entirely understand its import. We have all valued your very real, if unorthodox, approach to teaching, which has been something of a breath of fresh air. My wife and all your colleagues join me in wishing you every success in your work on applied philosophy, where your unconventional mode of addressing curriculum requirements will no longer be a handicap.

With warmest regards
Jim
(James Garner, MA, FSA)

And a deep sigh of cunicular relief – I could hear it esape when I opened the envelope. Somebody else could put him in a pie – I wouldn't.

My dear Son,

As you have probably heard, you were well out of England

161

during the last few weeks. That the Government in which we all placed so much faith should have failed so miserably to protect the City has been a great shock to us all. There was clearly foul play – orchestrated by the Americans, the Japanese and the Communists …

Separately or in concert? Read on.

but we all looked to Downing Street to forestall such activities – wrongly, it appears. Fortunately the Firm escaped – largely through the foresight of your friend Mr Sharkey. Although he left us before the blow fell, he had made our system fail safe, and it moved us into gold and Deutschmarks at exactly the right moment. I don't blame him for going where the grass is greener – I understand Logica has snapped him up. I don't much approve of headhunting, but he was loyal enough not to go to our competitors, and I respect that. Very probably he reckoned his work for us was finished, and I'd be the last to disagree. At least he taught us the uses of computers while the competition was floundering with them, and I'll be the first to acknowledge a debt to you – you introduced him. It may be the only thing you've been willing to do for your avaricious old father who doesn't reckon philosophy, but it was damned generous of you.

You also won't be surprised that the same avaricious old father has decided to call it a day. Two more years like last would shorten my life, which I don't at all appreciate. I am resigning at the end of the financial year in favour of young Briggs. You could have had the job if you had wanted it, but you probably prefer asking damn silly questions in an Irish bog. Your Mother is delighted, though that may not last when she has me under foot continually, and I intend to look into starting a small bookbinding business to avoid domestic trouble. She joins me in sending her love. If you want to be a philosopher, at least it helps to have a father who can finance the operation. I look forward to Sarah's future fecundity.

Your father.

P.S. They would visit us in Ireland and would I look into salmon fishing. Were there any decent hotels outside Dublin? Probably if and when Sarah was pregnant: I'd have to hide Sharkey if they did decide to visit, and put him up at the

Yeats Country Hotel. Unless there was certain pregnancy, Mother probably wouldn't come at the last moment.

We were going to buy a big old house on the Bay, with the ploughshare of Benbulbin pointing straight at it (Cynthia said it was a focus of power). It had been sacked in the Troubles, used as a holiday home for nuns, who'd put white paint over the stucco but left the brass chandeliers because they'd been made by a local ecclesiastical brassworker, and we were getting it cheap – chiefly because unlike some Germans who were after it, we would undertake not to close the footpaths across the demesne, make a fuss about grazing, or call the Gardai when some boys from the North practised musketry in the woods. Civilised behaviour, said Sharkey, would stop the neighbourhood gossiping about Matthew and make them rally round in emergency. It turned out, moreover, that Sharkey himself was a Sligo man. He also told me of a rather odd deal he and Cynthia had made with Antrobus: Antrobus had the idea of buying the QE2 as a floating business school for men only, chiefly Japanese. There were to be as many stewardesses, recruited mostly in Singapore, as students, and Cynthia was to train them. He was only waiting until there was a surefire cure for AIDS. Apparently Matthew, as a result of Enlightenment, didn't object – Cynthia was only to train them – and when I queried the matter with her, she said she felt a sense of obligation. Among the students there might be one or two susceptible to Enlightenment which would make the whole thing worthwhile: it was going to happen anyway, so why let it be demeaning and sordid? Moreover the ship wouldn't come anywhere near Ireland and destroy our welcome there, and Cynthia didn't think it would ever happen.

'And,' she said, 'it's more socially relevant than teaching the Whore's Ride to little live-in girlfriends as a present for their men. Sexuality can do so much more than that.'

'Well,' I said, 'you did a bloody good job with Sarah. *And* you got rid of a lot of her confidence problems: now she puts them down to being killed by the Nazis in the last war.'

'Oh yes,' said Cynthia, 'I can always spot an ancient soul.'

163

There was already a pile of rubble and paintpots at the foot of the carriage steps of Ballyconnell House. The painter and his apprentice were sitting eating sandwiches in a van.

'Is it a hotel they're making?'

'It's an office. They call it an Institute. Don't ask me what they're instituting because they didn't say.'

16

It was possible to work here before all the PCs were delivered. You could put the matter at issue into the slot on top of your brain, then walk for hours with Sarah along deserted beaches, covered with lines of weed, and watch the red and yellow snailshells roll down the dunes into bleaching piles in the hollows: after which, without prior warning, an answer – possibly the answer – would print out as a thought. This is how all abstract thinking works, in science, creative art, and philosophy, but there it was particularly conspicuous. Garner would have thought we were simply idle – for him the academic apparatus had to be making noises to be seen to be working – he'd trust computers only if they contained tangible cogwheels and emitted puffs of steam.

After about two months, with the plumbing operational, a generator installed, and a single cluster of furniture round a desk in each of the large eighteenth-century rooms, we too were operational. The residences upstairs in the old servants' quarters were comfortable, though the windows rattled. The Shark went back to London, sold my flat, had my effects packed, and came back in the second car, which the Institute would need. He seemed well pleased with what he saw: he gave the Government another couple of months before its own back benches hove it out, and he despatched copies of the other Institute's VIP Handbook to numerous Grocer-hostile destinations, 'just to grease the slipway'.

Tangible evidence of the Sharkey revolution was to be seen closer at hand. Shopping for the Institute in Sligo, Sarah and I passed two elephantine parked buses labelled 'YEATS COUNTRY TOUR' and packed with Euro-bourgeois. Each was in charge of a bookie-like courier with a fawn blazer, one haranguing his bus through a mike while the other had nipped out to urinate behind a wall. When the two of them reconvened for a consultation, I saw their faces. Familiar faces. Hatton and Thorburn, travel couriers – how are the snooty fallen, Hatton having trouble with his bladder through lack of advance planning, Thorburn trying to explain to a Belgian driver how to get his juggernaut to Lissadell. We crossed over deliberately and passed them as the colloquy broke up. They stopped and took me in, decided simultaneously that there was nothing to be ashamed of in honest work, and put on a tattered version of the old yuppie grin.

'Ah, David! Didn't expect to see you here. Prospering, I hope?' That was Hatton.

'Prospering,' I said. 'That's an original way of holding a financial planning seminar, carting it around the cultural landmarks in a bus.'

'Yes, well, it's not exactly a financial planning seminar, it's our bread and butter. Didn't you hear what happened?' said Hatton. 'Some buggers in Japan staged a bear raid on sterling – wouldn't have thought it possible; and our computer went down in the middle of it. I think we were nobbled.'

'So you're following the PM's advice in a new context?' I said.

'Don't follow you.'

'Well, it was the PM's idea to develop service industries at the expense of actually making things – become a nation of restaurateurs and brothel-keepers, or rather waiters and whores: I suppose that includes running bus tours.'

'Good, very good,' said Hatton, 'always taking the mickey, David.'

'No mickey, I'm serious. Who bought you the buses?'

'They're actually the property of a consortium,' said Hatton. Thorburn had come alongside. He said 'What Jojo means is that they belong to about fifteen Sikhs. The organising character's a chap who used to be a truck-driver. They got

166

Nobuo Myasaka to put up the capital and they bought the buses. We are now honestly employed.'

'Must feel better,' I said. 'What's the Sikh's name?'

'Well, they're all called Singh, aren't they?' said Hatton.

'What about the rest of his name? Is it Mansur Singh by any chance?'

'Something like that. Mansur Singh, Brothers and Partners.'

'Nice work,' I said, 'I know old Mansur.'

Sounds of bourgeois impatience in the buses.

'They seem to want you,' I said.

'Yes, we'd better get back to the chain gang. You look indecently prosperous,' said Hatton.

'I've got an Institute here, with friends.'

'But no manners – you didn't introduce us to the lady.'

'My wife – Sarah, meet two tradefallen yuppies, Mr Hatton and Mr Thorburn, late of the world of palmtrees, rubber plants and atria, now poodle-faking for a busload of Krauts.'

'I apologise for my husband,' said Sarah, 'I think that unkind remark was meant to be funny, not insulting.'

'Not to worry,' said Thorburn, 'it's bloody well true. See you in Hell, David – Mrs David.' And he got back on the bus.

Sharkey and Hamsen spent their days in what had been a small ballroom, sitting facing one another at PCs and as happy as sandboys. We mulled over the idea of Mind as 'the universe seeing itself', Spencer-Brown algebras, and the idea of re-entrant processing – after which the two gnomes would go back to their keyboards and play games with that. Sharkey also had a bulletin board on which he pinned up headlines from the remote British Press. At first they were routine:

NEW SCANDAL ROCKS CITY
MINISTER DEAD OF AIDS (*Times*)
BUGGER'S BLIGHT FELLS MINISTER (*Sun*)
PORKY: ONE BONK TOO MANY (*Daily Star*)

but soon they acquired substance:

167

HOMELESS STORM DOWNING STREET
ENOUGH IS ENOUGH
ON AND ON AND OUT

to which Sharkey added, underneath,

PM SEEKS ASYLUM WITH BOTHA

neatly simulated in stick-on letters. The process of terminal decay was too slow for him, but gradually the malodorous puffball was going back to compost. The Occupying Forces had something to occupy them, a collapsing Empire and now no home base to fall back on – the come-uppance of Babylonian proportions which had been so long delayed. Soon we'd be able to pull the chain, shut the lid and open the windows – but I was happy here.

I got another letter, an Oriental one.

Esteemed Mr David.

Forgive silence, I have only just got your address. You were very wise to get yourself out sharpish as there has been plenty of trouble – it did not touch me, however: I am well, and my esteemed wife has presented my third son, so I am most pleased.

Further there has been an intervention of good Providence. Two of my brothers were arrested by the police for driving unsafe vehicle. Being taken for defence fighters they were very much beaten by Police, in the thought that there were no witnesses. However this was an error, as the brutality was observed by a secretary woman and three honest Police. One of these being a Sikh was not believed by Commissioner, but the other two were Englishmen and they were believed. There is internal enquiry – on threat of great public disorder and riot, my brothers were recompensed with £25,000 having appeared on television telling their sufferings. This was worthwhile revenge, not having been seriously hurt, and with it we have bought a bus. My brothers had briefly to leave London, because certain misguided in our community insisted that the money should be given to Khalistan Freedom Fighters, but we thought this was neither wise nor necessary.

Having leased the bus and our services to a Japanese travel agency, they were pleased with our work and provide capital to buy further buses. There was trouble with the Race Relations Board who say we employ only Sikhs, but with more buses coming now over the Channel we have Belgian drivers also, and I am working in the offices and no more driving. Fortune is very transient, but we are so far rich, which is very nice and which we owe to beating by Police, in which we see the hand of God. Visit us soon to see the child and eat with us.

With brotherly sentiment
Jardan, Mansur Singh (Mr)

God moves in a mysterious way and even uses National Front coppers to prosper the righteous. We also heard from Sarkar, who'd gone back to teach at the Hindu University, saying that his brother had found favour in the eyes of Violet and they'd been married in South America. From now on she would run the Underground Railroad from the Indian and South American ends. Sarah was absolutely delighted. Violet said nothing about being shanghaied, so I reckoned that that was over.

We dispatched Sharkey to England, to see how the political fallout was progressing. While he was away there was a peculiar news story: it started with an explosion which damaged a house adjacent to an American air base, attributed officially to a gas leak: shortly after, a question in the House which raised the matter of accidental firing of a Sidewinder missile. This led to a violent shouting-match with the Prime Minister – the Hon Member was peddling anti-Americanism – and then a few days' preternatural silence, followed suddenly by a volley of injunctions against newspapers threatening to print a story on the affair. Our ears pricked: somebody was onto something which had the Occupying Power rattled, and it didn't sound like a misfired missile. We waited expectantly for Sharkey.

'Violet,' said Sharkey, 'can be grateful we exported her. That was a bunch of her little friends.'

'Doing what?'

'Bombing an American air base and knocking out three expensive F-111's on the ground. I wonder why I troubled to give seminars – if Violet had been around she would now be with her boyfriend.'

'They got nabbed?'

'They did. And don't ask me when the trial opens, because it won't open – that's what the security cover-up's about. We have Britain's first four desaparicidos.'

'Do you mean they just bumped them off?' said Sarah.

'Very possibly – or handed them over to the Americans,' said Sharkey.

'Have you evidence of this?' said Hamsen, swelling up with patriotic wrath. 'This happened when you were in England – you didn't by any chance instigate it, did you?'

Sharkey looked hurt. 'Prof, you know what I think of cowboy activists. This is precisely the kind of operation I'd expect of ninja motivated by what David calls inferior benevolence, in other words not enough between the ears. Quite bright ninja, mind you – it was a clever operation. They got an old furniture van and filled it with big black helium balloons. They waited for a night with a steady, stiff wind. They sent off a pathfinder balloon with a flashing LED on it, and had an observer outside the base with two-way radio to give them the wind speed. They hung small charges on the balloons, using thin nylon lines run through the fuses so that the charges would drop over the target, and they cut the fuses obliquely – they'd got them laid out in a bundle and measured so they could cut them and get a straddle. Numbers One and Two raised each balloon, Number Three lit the fuse, and off it went. Then they piled into the van and split. Six minutes later it rained bangers – mostly on target, but one overshot and hit a house: damn lucky it was empty, and no thanks to them.'

'Probably gave the Gallant Allies a fright,' I said.

'Bah!' said Sharkey. 'They could have done that with some clever jamming. Fault no. 1, it was an idiotic target. Terrorists haven't shifted any NATO bases by harassing them. Fault no. 2, after all that tactical planning they came home and told their friends, including twenty-odd hangers-on who'd attached themselves to the group: including, of course, the snout who had an eye on them. Quite apart from the fact that with a minor wind shift they could have wiped out a village.

And, of course, the basic weakness: it wasn't an operation to save mankind, it was a caper to make them feel good.'

'Whereas your subtler and less homicidal caper didn't make you feel good?' said Hamsen.

'I have no objection to a glow of satisfaction, but it has to be secondary to serious purpose,' said the Shark. 'I'm not sure we can even make use of the present cover-up: people don't like terrorists. Auntie Flossie might get wasted by a bomb on the Underground, and they deserve to be disappeared. Probably provide the Occupying Power with a useful diversion from the economic mess – save them looking for another colonial war. Why don't these people think?'

I thought Sharkey was hard on these Guy Fawkes conspirators. It was a natural enough reaction, and they'd twisted a few tails. I also thought that Sharkey was right. I was glad he'd fallen into my class, or there but for the grace of God.

'You seem to know a dickens of a lot about it,' said Hamsen.

'I have sources,' said the Shark, 'after all, intelligence is our business, isn't it? I think, on consideration, we can communicate the facts to a few MPs. We'll leave it to them to decide on making use of it.'

17

We'd been going about six months when I saw a soutane coming up the drive in the rain. Malachi looked older, more clerical – he shut his umbrella and rang the Institute doorbell. We didn't have sufficient visitors to warrant a receptionist. I let him in.

'So I've run you to earth,' said Malachi. 'Is Matthew here?'

'Not here, exactly – he's up at the cottage.'

'How is it with him?' said Malachi.

'Very well, mentally and spiritually.'

'I'm glad of that.'

'You haven't by any chance come to recall him to duty?' I said.

'Not at all, but I'm the man's friend. Should I go there, or will he be coming here?'

'I'll run you up. Have coffee first.'

Sharkey was delighted to see him and for once didn't let his coffee get cold. Hamsen, who didn't know him, was suspicious of the dog-collar, but warmed to Malachi. Sarah looked, well, a little vigilant, but welcoming. Malachi finished his coffee, expressed a wish to be off on his pastoral visit, so I brought the old VW round, and we bumped off towards the cloud-topped knife of Benbulbin, creased by small streams that drain the tabletop.

I didn't go in with him. He stayed an hour.

When he came out, he said, 'It's as you told me. God wasn't about to lose his priest.'

'He doesn't see himself as a priest,' I said.

'Ah, but he is,' said Malachi. 'There's more than one kind of priest. The woman brought him closer to where he had to go, not further from it.'

'You won't set the hierarchy on him, I gather.'

'It's not for me to interfere with that, nor for them.'

'Because a spoiled priest wouldn't go down well here ...'

'I know it, I'm an Irishman. But Matthew is no spoiled priest. He looked for his vocation in the ordinary place, and it was the wrong place for him. That woman might have spoiled me if I'd been susceptible, but she's carried Matthew forward. Now tell me,' said Malachi, 'what you're doing with those machines of yours.'

'It's technical, padre.'

'Don't underrate yourself. I attended your classes.'

'Well,' I said, 'we wanted to start by seeing how Mind builds up a universe.' He nodded. 'We started with the idea of Mind as reflexive, and we're using line automata to generate fractals based on recurrent equations, starting with some of the strings in Programme Universe theory – the extension of S-matrix theory. We want to see what kind of structures that generates.'

'And after that?'

'See what happens with non-Kantian models.'

'In that case,' said Malachi, 'you've got the better of elapsing time?'

'We haven't. Line automata display in time. Time's the bugger of it.'

'Time's the source of it,' said Malachi, 'and God doesn't deal in it, for my money.'

'You're probably right.'

'You might as well know,' said Malachi, 'that my cure of souls extends to philosophy. I'm to teach it at Maynooth. I expect to shake them, all those little Thomists. Thanks to your able instruction.'

'Cynthia could do it quicker,' I said.

'Don't suggest it. That's not the way we play it in the Christian Church.'

'Why not?'

'Well, it's not in the regimental drill book.'

'You may shake their ideas up,' I said, 'but there's not much in our thinking that would have any relevance at all to Christian theology. Buddhist, yes – Christian, no. It's a different order of discourse. Except panavatarism – that Buddhahood is in all of us.'

'It's good doctrine that God is in all of us unless we kick him out,' said Malachi, 'and that's not easy to do.'

I asked him if he thought that made us the equals of Christ in a minor way.

'His brothers, by his own saying,' said Malachi, 'not his equals. Anyway, there are other things in us beside a portion of divinity, or the implicate, or whatever your Gnostics call it. Does your Buddhism have a doctrine of evil?'

'As I see it,' I said, 'Buddhist philosophers put evil down to involvement – taking the virtual world as real. They cure it by Enlightenment, not salvation.'

'Then there you're wrong, in our book,' said Malachi, 'unless the two are the same. You'll not make a Gnostic out of me, for that reason alone. And it seemed to me that you and the rest of them took evil seriously enough when you set out to play hell with the greedy and uncaring. Seriously enough to be angry, and that's a non-Buddhist emotion. What you call inferior benevolence. Do you not want to enlighten the Grocer?'

'Yes, and I'd like to erotise the state of Kansas, but it's hard sledding. You can slip back from being human if you don't keep climbing. I'm just about tired with being angry,' I said, 'I don't remember a time when I wasn't bloody mad with what some bastard or other was doing to his neighbours. Probably do it myself without noticing.'

'You probably do. I'll prescribe a penance if you like.'

We got back to the house. I think the others were a little apprehensive about what Malachi might have been up to with Matthew, but I signalled that all was well. Malachi not only stayed to lunch – he argued with Hamsen about recursive algebras and the lapse of time and let Sharkey take him off to punch keys on the PC and watch physical form evolving from algorithms.

174

'Clever chap,' said Hamsen, 'much as I distrust priests. Not really lucid. They've got an agenda to prove – even when they get some vision in spite of themselves, they insist on marching in lead boots. That's why they're so obstinately celibate. A woman might make them think dangerously, huh?'

Sharkey pinned up another headline on the board:

CHAOS SWEEPS SCHOOL SYSTEM

He looked extremely self-satisfied.

'Let's take bets,' said Hamsen. 'A fiver says it will take the Papal Academy fifty years to come to terms with physics.'

'No takers,' said Sarah. 'We won't most of us be here to collect.'

'What I'm waiting for,' said Hamsen, 'is the first hint of extraterrestrial intelligence. That'll put the cat among the atonement theorists. Did Christ die for the universe, or only for Man? I'm also waiting for the first celestial object with a Hubble number greater than the age of the universe. That'll put a pussy amongst the physicists. Hubble's due for retirement, unless I'm much mistaken. Arp thinks so.'

Cynthia stuck a damp head round the door. 'Has he gone?' she said.

'Not yet – he's in the ballroom with the Shark.'

'Well, he put Matthew's mind at rest – it's the one extra thing he needed.'

I told her we'd just been hearing the moderate Catholic position.

'Malachi won't *stay* there,' said Cynthia.

'Do you think you could help him?

She shook her head. 'Wrong sadhana – he's got his own. We all must have. But either he'll shape up, or do it next time around. A life as a woman wouldn't hurt him,' she said. 'He's on his way. I can see that.'

I offered to run Malachi back to the Sligo road to get the bus, but it had stopped raining, Benbulbin was slaty-grey and steaming, and we decided to walk. We took the short cut

175

through the old walled garden, now being rehabilitated by me, by Sarah, and by Sharkey. Malachi trudged down the path.

'You have a power of vegetables there,' he said. 'Any philosophical significance?'

I explained that forming ideas was like pig-rearing – it's slow and happens out of sight: you prod them occasionally to see if they're ready for market, and in the meantime you grow vegetables or do something else useful. Constant argument interferes with what is going on down there among the neurones.

'You've discovered that technique,' said Malachi. 'Monks have done it for a long time. I wish poets would – I mean, work at something useful while the mixer's running, instead of sitting jawing in Mooney's.'

Meanwhile, I agreed, we must cultivate our garden. The preconscious is our greatest resource, and we might as well let it do its own work.

'Half time as the ninja, half time as the bodhisattva, you said, didn't you, David?'

I told him it was a workable mix, and we'd get there eventually, though whether ideas work better than throwing-stars was an open question.

'I think probably they do,' said Malachi. 'Would that be the way up to the bus?'

176